Mera F

Four Years of Stupidity, Madness and Brilliance

**Dhirendra Mishra &
Himanshu Shekhar Dutta**

INDIA · SINGAPORE · MALAYSIA

Notion Press Media Pvt Ltd

No. 50, Chettiyar Agaram Main Road,
Vanagaram, Chennai, Tamil Nadu – 600 095

First Published by Notion Press 2021
Copyright © Dhirendra Mishra & Himanshu
Shekhar Dutta 2021
All Rights Reserved.

ISBN 978-1-63957-555-8

This book is dedicated to students who never compromise on fun even if it comes at the expense of studies.

Contents

Foreword

Mera Bhi Proxy Maar Dena is a nostalgic, hilarious and fascinating depiction of the most exhilarating years of a student's life.

Like almost every student who's passed through this Engineering College, I too have fond memories of NIT Rourkela, Odisha (then REC Rourkela and a graduate programme of 5 years). I know this book will bring anyone who's been a student, not just of NIT, to reminisce about their most exceptional years – the ones spent in college. Three cheers to endless discussions and nostalgic memories. Steve Jobs said, 'The Journey is the reward'. I would add: The Journey from 'Back post' to classrooms was equally memorable and rewarding...

– **CP Gurnani**

Acknowledgments

The four NIT Rourkela years passed by. And years later, got penned. A feat for sure! Every object—living and non-living in and around the college and hostel—had its share of contribution in the realization of this feat. We thank our NIT Rourkela batch for being a conglomerate of variety. But for this variety, this book would not have been possible. Special thanks to the *Electrical* class of this batch.

We are indebted to **Keshto**, the *chai* man at the hostel canteen; **Pattani Babu**, the *chana* man who would walk around the boys' hostels getting us something, at least something to munch; the **Backpost**, that gave some respite to our hungry bellies when our taste buds could bear no more of the hostel food. We are obliged to the *Jurassic Park* behind the Boys Hostel that was home to snakes, insects and rodents that would sneak into the hostel corridors giving us boys something to talk and shout about. The TV in the hostel common room that would telecast just the one channel (DD1 Doordarshan)... the one Table Tennis table in each hostel with 300 boys... the hundreds of in-ICU (in bad shape) bicycles in the hostel bicycle parking lot... the hostel that stayed awake 24 X 7... and many more. We took everything for granted then. 25 years later, driving down the memory lanes, we have realized how much we have missed them all.

We thank our friends **Swayam Prakash Mishra, Rajesh Ivaturi, Nishant Sharma, Ambika Das** and **Himanshu Tripathi** for sharing their thoughts that helped in enriching the book content. Our friends and alumni **Ayaskant Kanungo, Abhijit Bhadra** and **Dushyant Mishra** had great ideas to contribute in adding value to the book. Special thanks to **Vinith Acharya** and **Prathik Acharya** for adding lively illustrations. Vinith was exemplary in deducing the look, feel, gait, and grace of the characters, be it *Kehsto's, Pattani Babu's* , or *Prof. Mohanty's*!

In writing down these stories, we traveled back in time to be students yet again; living in the hostel and living life again. Thanks to the world that the students make: the liveliest and the most happening.

And thanks in advance to all who will read this book.

****

I would be in the middle of a story; all engrossed in the Rourkela memories; smiling to myself, at times laughing. Sweta would pass by and I would narrate everything to her. The story writing went on for months and Sweta lent her patient ears to my narration all along. Poor lady! Ankit would be just done with his school assignments and I would spend some time convincing him that he was a great reviewer and that he could add value to my story by reviewing it all. And he would be bang on every time.

Sweta and Ankit, this collection would have been so scrappily incomplete without your contributions.

I would like to thank my brothers, Dr. Dharmendra Kr. Mishra and Mr. Ragendra Mishra for having been my guides, mentors and sources of inspiration from the day I came into this world. Your inputs and best wishes in the making of this book were priceless. And then my parents. They say *it ends where it started from.* Thanks to Mrs. Shakuntala Mishra and Mr. Shyam Deo Mishra for being there by my side. Even when the Sun goes to the other side of the globe and darkness descends on this side, you have been there for me; keeping it all bright for me. Thank you again.

– Dhirendra Mishra

****

I would like to thank my wife, Susmita and our sons, Mayank and Vedant. I would also like to take a moment to remember my parents, Late Indra Deo Dutta and Late Leela Dutta who are always with me and my family. My family and my work won't be complete without mentioning my sisters, Aruna, Bandana and Archana and my brothers, Ashutosh, Bibhutosh and Sudhanshu.

– Himanshu Shekhar Dutta

Introduction

As though a few cans of grease had tumbled on **Time**, the four Rourkela years went *quick* and *slippery*. *Quick* because of the semester system where a semester would end even before one could recover from the aftershock of the previous which one had taken a resolve to do better. *Slippery* because the resolutions could not stick and life never steadied. Considering the efforts the boys had put in the run-up to the admission at the college, everyone including parents had some visuals in mind about how studiously hectic the four-year Engineering College life would be. Hectic the boys sure remained all four years. But studiously?

Most boys and girls were living the dreams of their parents when they first arrived at Rourkela. The grandness of the dreams showed on the faces of accompanying parents who were proud to have been living that dream 'today'. All these years, they had shown loads of gratitude to other parents who were *modest* when their kids got into Engineering. These same parents were cross with many others who reflected *arrogance* when their kids had made their way into Engineering. And 'today' when these parents instead had the choice of being *modest* or *arrogant*, their happiness and contentment knew no bounds.

The four Rourkela years were vibrant and replete with *undulating rhythms* and *distinctive flavors*. The *rhythms* and *flavors* were not about singing aloud in joy after a sumptuous meal but rather about swearing at the lousy hostel meals every day! They were not about making amends for a disastrous semester result by working harder as much they were about complaining, criticizing and condemning a rather 'faulty system' that had made a mockery of intelligent students!

The boys and the girls alike could conquer the degree in four years. What they could not, however, was the dilemma over whether the stay was more about *fun* or *slog*. If one moment was all about *concerns*, the very next would be all about *taking things easy* because many more were on the same boat. Overall, all four years of life in Rourkela went into planning about getting 'a touch more serious from tomorrow' and discovering as many times that 'tomorrow' never came. The first four semesters went into believing that the 'campus placement and job' season was far away and that there was ample time to catch up. Until one fine day, the realization dawned that 'my calculations' ought to have been a touch more frugal and realistic!

The Rourkela innings was more about the *paths* I believed the horizon would open for me than the *roads* I could see. More about the *wheels* that could turn than the *cogs* that could slow them down. The four years were more about *instincts* that made me believe that I could do than the *proof* that the world claimed having done. The stay was more about the *empirical* that got me to build castles in the air than *priori* that constructed the Great Wall of China. Many years into the end of the most prolific four years, as I lean back, I can hear the wind with specks of chirps and flutters rustling through my ears, calling me, speaking in a language I can recognize but voices I cannot identify. I know them all. And as Rourkela calls, I cannot wait to see them all...

Year I: Started with a Flicker; Ended with a Flash

College Bund Karane Ke Nuskhe

Sai and I shared the same room in our 1st year hostel stay, with Shivram and Prabhu filling the remaining corners. Come evening and Sai would often become *Bhang*-ed[1]. It is said that excessive consumption of *Bhang* in one go gets the better of one's abilities to stop doing what one has been doing. Laugh and you will keep laughing; cry and you will keep crying. Sai was no exception. Euphoria one evening and despair the other was how Bhang would show on Sai. Under the bout of euphoria, Sai would laugh, and laugh as

---

1 *Bhang* is a weed. It comes from the leaves and flower tops of a plant from the family called cannabis. People consume it in many ways. The recreational form, eaten in raw form or drunk with milk is *Bhang*. The narcotic form is smoked and is called Ganja.

though there would be no tomorrow. Under despair, he would cry. And cry as though the world was coming to an end. Anyone *Bhang*-ed gave ample time for all spectators around him to enjoy the fun. This was because it took reasonably long to get over this high. Sai, again, was no exception!

The 1st year was when we were under the spell of black magic: ragging. Any Tom, Dick, or Harry from the senior batches would often enter the 1st year hostel rooms and thrash any of us as much as he liked. Another lot would then have their share of musings. And therefore, at a time when the seniors' thrashings and musings were bigger causes of concern for us 1st year boys, abnormalities such as those of Sai remained unnoticed. Or at most, the least talked about.

One day, the 1st year students were issued marching orders by the seniors to ready themselves for a protest march. Those were the anti-Mandal days, and the march was aimed at declaring to the city police (and the world) that the Mandal Commission implementation was unacceptable. This implementation had to do with reservations in government jobs for the OBCs (Other Backward Classes) to the tune of 27% and to which the population showing in the General category had strong reservations against. Although the march was apparently a 'protest', only the students knew the real reasons. It had been a tried and tested formula over the last few years in college that any such protest march got the police to intervene. Fearing that such protest marches could eventually lead to violence and unrest in the city, the police would then declare a hostel sine-die, meaning that the hostel and the college would remain closed until further notice. And this 'further notice' usually came after considerable time, very easily a month. The 1ˢᵗ year students did not have the option to say no to the marching orders from the seniors. The protest was all about the 1ˢᵗ year students with only a handful from the senior batches. And those from the senior batches were there only to ascertain that the march ended in a rather long college vacation!

On this occasion though, the college management could smell a rat and was successful in thwarting the protest march attempt. The management's timely crackdown split the hostel crowd even before all could assemble. The boys had to rush for cover and back they ran to their hostel rooms even before the protest slogans could start airing!

A livid college Dean (one Prof. Ganguly), a usually-serene-but-far-from-it-now Hostel Warden (Prof. Damodar) and one junior professor entered our hostel. The junior professor too wore an angry face to show his senior counterparts that this was indeed unacceptable. "How dare these puppies barked this loud?" was the expression the fast walking Prof. Ganguly and his coterie wore as they decided to run amok in the hostel. Banging into every hostel room one after the other, the three literally tore us apart. Four seaters that the 1ˢᵗ year hostel rooms were, one bang into a room got them to vent a heart-full of fury and fire that the four occupants could burn under at one time. Declaring that 'such misadventures' were far from acceptable in a college that had boasted of saints up until then, this group of three could make many of the hostelers believe that they had indeed stooped low by having attempted the protest that day! The Dean in particular declared loud and clear that timely reparation was all that could spare us, "or else…" By the time the team ran past three to four rooms in the hostel, news spread that a trio had entered the hostel and that it was just about the time that 'we fastened our seat belts!' There were two groups in the hostel: One that had been sermoned by the trio and who Prof. Ganguly and team thought was quarantined and the other who was about to be. The 'about to be quarantined' group included our room. This group waited for their turn as though a vaccine was about to be administered in the form of an injection. Their expressions and mood said it all.

It was a matter of time when the quarantine group banged our door. Prof. Ganguly and his crew entered room no. 30 of Hostel I. The inmates—four silly goats—stood up with heads down as though they had been party to the biggest crime of the millennium and to which they weren't denying having been part of. Our biggest concern at that moment, however, was not about how discordant a trumpet Ganguly and team would blow. Far from it, it was how terrible our fourth silly goat, Sai, would dance to their tune. Yes, Sai was *Bhang*-ed that night and was crying inconsolably when the gang entered our room. The 'Sai cry' sounded to the squad like the cry of the wolves and fortunately for us remaining three, the guns were all pointing at him. "You come to the college for hooliganism, not studies, and cry ashamedly at being outsmarted." "You all…" and the guns turned to us too as Prof. Ganguly and his entourage were now on their way out of Room no. 30 and ready to enter Room no. 31, "…are just one misadventure away from what could be curtains to your Rourkela stay. I repeat, just one away…"

It was now the turn of the silly goats in Room no. 31 to hear Prof. Ganguly's trumpets. When this was 'in progress', we rejoiced; jumping and celebrating in delight that our Sai was 'crying' that day when the professors came in. "Thank God," we said, "Sai was not laughing non-stop today as he occasionally does when Bhang-ed." If that were the case, Prof. Ganguly might well have taken the law into his hands and possibly slaughtered the silliest of the room no. 30 goats that day! Sai had a reprieve and we, a story…

Tooti Deewar, Nikla Backpost

If a pie were to be drawn to represent all problems bothering the hostel boys, 'terrible hostel food' would so very easily show a lion's share on it. Sniffing around the neighborhood for some respite, the *bhookad* boys would hear The **Backpost** calling!

The **Backpost** was that area behind the far east of the college campus, adjoining the Boys Hostel. Come evening and the hostel boys would swarm around in bunches, reaching the **Backpost** for some intake that the yelling box (the stomach) had been long demanding. The **Backpost** delicacies included *Guptaji's* **aloo paratha**, *Mahesji's* **Maggi**, *Panda Babu's* **samosa**, to name a few. On the whole, the Backpost was about the hut remains, the thatched roofs, the small village boys running around with tiny clanging bells hanging by black threads around their waist, most likely to shield them from black magic and evil spirits. The **Backpost** was also about a variant of Hindi that one doesn't hear anywhere else in the world—a touch coarser than the already-coarse variant spoken elsewhere in Rourkela. It was where— irrespective of whether you chose *Mahesh's* or *Gupta's* or *Panda's* on an evening—you would not release all your weight on the chairs or benches you sat on until you were sure that it would withstand you without giving in! The **Backpost** was more to feel and less to see; still lesser to describe. On the whole, **Backpost** was more than the sum of its parts. It was symbolic of 'casual' and one ad-line that suited it more than any else was Jockey's: *Next to nothing!* No wonder, the hostel boys could settle for nothing less than being in **love** with it.

A **wall** stood between the college campus and the **Backpost**, characteristic enough that a barrier is always in the destiny of those who **love**. A three-foot-wide passage through the wall connecting the hostel arena to the Backpost—and that was years old— demonstrated the fact that in a showdown between **love** and wall, **love** wins and the wall gets razed. Interestingly, the wall flanges along the extracted wall bricks had long gotten over the scars of the raze and was testimony to the fact that the hostel boys' affair with the **Backpost** dated back to tens of years!

Guptaji at the **Backpost** had two specialties: one which the boys were interested in: the Aloo Paratha, and the other which Guptaji was himself in: Mrs. Gupta. No wonder, Guptaji had a strong contingent of children at home. It was said that **Guptaji** himself had lost the count of them, let alone their names! While chopping vegetables that were to be served with aloo paratha, Guptaji, crisscrossing his arms over his shoulders, would more often than not run the knife blade against his own back to oblige to the itch that dared him more often than not! Aloo paratha, kids, Mrs. Gupta, itch and what more, Guptaji had to be a busy man!

Maheshji held a diploma in Maggi making. Simultaneously juggling with a few single-burner kerosene stoves and as many pans, Maheshji doled out Maggi in '2 minutes' indeed and no more! In came a shout from the boys, "Maheshji, 4 by 5," and he would be on course to prepare four Maggi packets to serve five boys. "Maheshji, 2 by 3" would be another call for Maheshji to quell three hungry bellies very soon, this time from two Maggi packets. And the distribution across the plates would be so equal; one could pick a plate with eyes closed!

And there was a Panda Babu, an expert in samosas. They said he was a Ghosh and not Panda but carried on the legacy of his father-in-law who happened to be Pandaji. Come evening, the entire Panda family would be at work: Panda Babu and his wife stuffing, sealing and frying samosas and his teen daughters serving those. The samosas were good but that was not the sole reason why the hostel boys rushed to Panda's joint! From time to time, Panda Babu would go around with that black six-cup tea holder in his right hand, collecting the soiled cups with his left. His hurriedness—and this showed writ on his face during peak hours—indicated how he wished he had at least one more hand if not two to make up for the lag between demand and delivery!

To the hostel boys, months of slogging had marked the beginning of the rat race that they thought would end once they made it to the engineering college. But having got there, they realized that the race was far from over. Worse still, the boys were just not able to determine where the race was leading. And in that never-ending race as though set in a desert, the **Backpost** was like an oasis that helped breathe some air into the lives of the hostel boys. Overall, more than a place, the Backpost was an emotion that the boys could flow in and out with.

Mess Ka Khana? Aaj Nahi Yaar…

The quality of hostel food bears a strong relation to the restaurant business around. And when the hostel is fairly large as REC Rourkela's and the town as small as Rourkela's, every good restaurant in the town can attribute a fair share of its business to the hostel boys. The notable restaurants and the eating joints in the town were **Mandap**, the **Taste**, the **Madhuban**, the **Radhika**, the **Mayflower** and the count ran out. The occasion, the pocket, the mood, the means of commute and the sick-of-hostel-food syndrome—the mix of these were prime reasons why a reasonable count of the hostel boys thronged the restaurants just about every day. A good sumptuous lunch or dinner at a restaurant would calm down cravings for outside food for a while for at least two reasons. One, continuous hostel food would fill the tummy but lend serious disservice to the taste buds and with time, the taste buds could take no more of it. The second reason had to do with affordability. The ever-cash-strapped hostel boys had to factor in expenses too. Therefore, there had to be a cap on outside food!

The one no-occasion place where the boys could walk by without much thought was the **Backpost**. This was right beside the boys' hostels. Though it was an oasis of sorts in a desert, the **Backpost** had limitations in terms of variety. *Samosa, chai, Maggi, vada pav* and there ended the story. By and far, the **Backpost** was a welcome respite from the same-old-story hostel food without doubt, but this could at the most be a respite; not more. Next came the **Mandap**. A step-by-step review would place **Mandap** slightly ahead of **Backpost** in the rating list. One reason why **Mandap** looked ahead in the race was that it could boast of a 'menu' unlike the **Backpost** outlets. Lassi and Chowmein on the menu made **Mandap** way more cosmopolitan. But also true was the fact that **Mandap** ran short of various other delicacies including samosas and vada pav. What then gave **Mandap** the edge? The fact that college girls visited the **Mandap** made up for every other shortcoming. The Ladies Hostel would shut at seven-thirty in the evening. And the fact that there was no other similar hangout place within walking distance of the college made **Mandap** the default choice for the girls who hanged out. And consequently of the boys whom they hanged out with! Overall, **Mandap** was a hangout place more like the modern-day CCD (Café Coffee Day). Between **Backpost** and **Mandap**, if **Backpost** was *Rangeela Ka* Amir Khan, the **Mandap** was, well, the *Raja Hindustani wala*!

One fact associated with **Mandap** was that it was right beside the College Main Entrance just outside the college campus. As a result, others going out from or returning to the college/hostel would catch sight of the **Mandap** attendees. The severe scarcity of girls in the college got the boys to be extra-possessive and extra-vigilant about them and finding one in the company of some boy at **Mandap** would be a hostel best-seller (story) for a few days. How many days this story would sell best in the hostel depended on the boy-girl pair. **Manthra** in the company of **Arjun**[2] or **Johnny L** in the company of **Aish**[3] would take the hostel by a 'more furious' storm! The story gave good free publicity to the boy who was seen in the girl's company and he would not clarify much for that could well take the sheen off the publicity!

Backpost and **Mandap** were walking distance from the Boys Hostel. Anything else required added planning. The **Taste** was the next on the list. Reasonably good in taste and pocket, its drawback was the rush and consequently the wait time. The fact that it was a closed roof with running fans at the most, the place was generally hot and sultry. And though

2 Reference: Ramayana/Mahabharata
3 Reference: Bollywood

appearing in the list of possible go-to places to eat, it remained an option at the most, not a favorite. A/C restaurants were not typical those days and any in Rourkela that could boast of one would suck the hole out of your pocket!

Radhika for price and **Mayflower** for both price and distance from the hostel could not make it to the REC Rourkela list. With reasons ranging from elimination, relativity and absolutism, the one restaurant that remained ten times more visited than all others combined was the **Madhuban**. **Madhuban** was to the REC Rourkela hostel boys what Paracetamol is to fever; what Vim is to washing liquid; what Surf is to detergent and what Dettol is to antiseptic. From birthday treats to TTMM (Tera Tu Mera Main, where you would pay for yours; I for mine), **Madhuban** was the answer. From "hostel-*khana-se-pak-gaya-hoon* (fed up with hostel food)" to "the year-long effort to take her out that has finally materialized today," **Madhuban** was that panacea, truly unparalleled! On factors ranging from price to variety and from ambiance to style, **Madhuban** fitted the REC boys like a cork!

Not on *monumental* value but definitely on the *manobal* (morale), the **Madhuban** to the REC boys was no less than what the Taj Mahal has been to the Agra-ites! Many years after the last summer in Rourkela, when we recall the niceties of the town without which the fun-filled Rourkela years would not have been the same, **Madhuban** figures in just about everyone's list. We particularly remember the Chicken *Latpat* for Rs. 35 that we would share amongst three and that would recharge us to withstand all hostel meals for the coming three weeks. It was truly that special recharge that would take care of any and every incoming hostel-food-onslaught for three weeks!

Padhai Kal Kar Lena Yaar

The college auditorium had a fancy name, **AV Hall**, thanks to the official one-movie-per-week that showed on the 70mm screen. In the days when the internet was for the privileged few, the AV Hall movies were a rare and valued source of entertainment the hostel boys could not miss no matter what season of the year or semester it was. It would be a Hindi movie one week followed by an English one the next. The Hindi movies showing in the hall were usually the ones to have outlived their commercial value in the outside world. Most of the boys would have already watched the movie in the theatres elsewhere but that never came in the way of these boys watching the movie again when it showed in the AV Hall. As for any English movie, the boys would still flock to the AV Hall and make it houseful. For three reasons:

- the movie was for free

- not watching an English movie ran the risk of you being considered outdated. In line with,

"Who Rohan? That guy who does not watch English movies?"

- the boys sat through the English movies in the hope of some adult scenes which the Hindi movies were somehow so allergic to and bereft of

It was a different matter altogether that a majority of the crowd watching English movies made very little sense of what was going on. Now and then there would be some laughter in the hall. When you asked your neighboring guy who was also laughing, as to what made everyone laugh, the curtains would come off the reality: he would be laughing just because others were! The management's decision to have two shows per movie—one for the girls and the other for the boys—was the only reality associated with the AV Hall movies that the hostel boys disapproved of. And the intensity this disapproval carried was a fair indicator of why the management decided that way! The movie was *Dil Hai Ki Manta Nahi* wherein the actress Pooja (Pooja Bhatt) having run away from home to marry a film star, met Amir en route. While at Amir's place, her query inquiring where the **bathroom** was, got the entire hostel boys to be on their feet. The one voice in the AV Hall, however, that outpowered and outdid every other murmur was: "Hostel II!" In addition to such comments and running commentaries, the hostel boys had developed a style of appreciating the art called movies in a way only they could. The rule was simple and yet full-proof; years and years that it had taken to evolve: *If you noticed* *the movie screen shake, it was definitely hit by a piece or pair of footwear and if you weren't the one to hit, check if your footwear was around!* Emotions ran high in the AV Hall. No wonder when Anil Kapoor hugged Madhuri, a boy ran down to the screen to whip the screen with his belt; furiously enough to tear the screen apart! The screen-whipping-and-tearing incident meant that the always-poor hostel boys had to live with larger holes in their pockets the following month when the next installment of the college fees had the screen-tearing-penalty included. Yes, for all the boys!

They say script, music, actors and directors make a movie. At the AV Hall though, it was the atmosphere. What made the AV Hall movies so popular amongst the hostel boys was the lack of other entertainment sources at that time. Smartphones and internet-in-pocket were light-years away and had not even figured in dreams until then. Cable TV had started to reach select homes in the town but the reason it had not reached our hostels yet was that our college management believed that the M and F TVs could erode the ethos and family values in the boys that their parents had toiled hard to inject. We only had the DD Channels DD1 and DD2 running on our hostel TV. The management was of the view that DD1 and DD2 were at most *homeopathy* medicines that would not have side effects even if those did not instill great values in the students. But the likes of the channels that Cable TV brought, they believed, could be an overdose of an allopathy antibiotic that the 'young' hostel boys were not ready for yet! No wonder, in such a desert, the AV Hall was the symbol, or rather an oasis to fulfill desires. After all, the **Krishi-Darshan**, the **Jaan Hei Jahan Hei**, and the **Chitrahaar** romantic numbers (the programs that were telecast on Doordarshan) from the '60s fell far short of any such teen's whims and wishes!

Mrityunjay capitalized on these frantic teen desires when he laid his election manifesto. Yes, there would be an AV Hall secretary elected from amongst the 3rd year students, whose responsibility was to oversee the working of the AV hall. This included working with the distributors to arrange for the movies to show in the AV Hall. No wonder Mrityunjay won the election and it was time to come right on the poll promises. And Mrityunjay did not disappoint. In probably less than a month after he took office, came the sizzling *Power Play*. With the skin show as never before, the audience went berserk. With the AV hall deluged in the once-more chant at regular intervals and to which the projector boy had every reason to oblige, the movie took a good five hours to complete! The mood amongst the hostel boys was that of real freedom. India won freedom in Aug 1947, but the hostel boys could feel real freedom for the first time close to 50 years later!

The management reprimanded Mrityunjay and stripped him of his post of AV Hall secretary. But it was too small a price to pay for the clouds he thought he could burst in the desert!

Mere Se Nahi Bunn Padega

The year was 1996. India was playing Sri Lanka in the ICC World Cup Semi-Final. And the Sri Lankan bowlers were spitting fire. Indian batters were battered and the hostel common room where we boys were watching the match live on television sounded as silent as grave. A cricket match involving India was not just a sporting event; it was life and death for we hostel boys. Virdi appeared on the scene and asked if Sunil Gavaskar was yet to bat. It had been nine years since Gavaskar retired, and to escape the wrath of a crowd soaked in fury at a question as stupid, someone had to be unduly naïve and charming. Virdi was!

Once news broke that an ex-Indian prime minister, Morarji Desai, passed away. Virdi overheard a group of Andhra boys—college called this group 'Gulti'—discussing the possible postponement of the viva voce scheduled for the following day. Virdi came to tell us that some 'Gulti' leader had passed away (Morarji Desai hailed from Gujarat).

On the whole, Virdi was oblivious to the activities around the globe. But he more than made up for this ignorance by deciding to be next-only-to-Benjamin-Franklin in topics related to electrical engineering. His focus in electrical engineering was Arjun-like and combined with a bubbly charm, he made a lovable presence in the batch. Virdi was a Sardar (Punjabi) and that complemented his personality. Many a time, he would narrate stories when he would have been at the receiving end, but the child-like innocence he would exuberate at such narrations made the audience ask for more!

Once he went to buy underwear. He inquired about the price and the salesgirl replied, "Rs. 50." Virdi inquired about another piece. It was for Rs. 35. Virdi asked to pack the latter at which the salesgirl said, "*Wo Ladki ka hai* (those are girls')." The blush that Virdi would have worn in front of the salesgirl and the same that he exhibited while narrating that story and many more similar instances, made everyone around fond of him.

Virdi was a born story maker. He would not write stories but his presence got the air around to create stories! Those were the 1st year hostel days. And he happened to occupy the hostel room right next to mine. His roommate Pranav came to us asking for a plier. He came back again a while later, this time checking for a screwdriver. He was not third time lucky either when he asked for a hammer. With strange asks unbecoming of what the hostel boys would generally ask for, our curiosity reached the threshold. We came to know that Virdi's leather belt around his waist had locked 'permanently' and any amount of effort ranging from the soft jerks and shakes on the buckle all the way to the soft plier and hard hammer blows could not budge the buckle. Virdi was lying flat on his bed facing the roof, in a state of shock, when we entered his room.

Virdi's zip worked fine. More importantly, he had relieved himself from the big one early in the morning even before trying the belt. So the situation was not that bad. But then in life, how severe your problem is cannot be judged by others; instead it is how you feel about it. And going by Virdi's expressions and body language, his problem was monumental; the terrorized look on his face said it all. This partly stemmed from the fact that his other two roommates Prasanna and Jayant had just, after getting him to lie on the bed, tried pulling his pants down with all their might, hoping that the persistent and stubborn belt would come rolling down with the pant. Not to be. Prasanna and Jayant would have tried some more but Virdi stopped them. For at least two reasons: i) it was hurting around his waist ii) he could hear some pant stitches coming undone!

A plier, screwdriver, hammer and more were used but nothing worked. Then why not scissors? To our questions, Virdi looked disinterested as much as he was exhausted. We left his room letting Virdi come to terms with the tremors he had still not got over. Pranav then told us that Virdi's London wali *bua* (aunt) had gifted him this 'imported' belt during her recent trip to India. We understood a world:

- 'Imported' that he presumed the belt was, Virdi could not approve of scissors being run on it

- That every *bua* usually buys gifts from the Saraojini Nagar market no matter where in the world she claims having brought them from

- Catastrophic it could be if zips too, like belts, were not an organic part of trousers!

What made Virdi popular and liked by all in the hostel was that he could get over such apparent traumas in very little time. You meet him the following morning at the breakfast table and he would be all fresh, joyful, excited and beaming with many more stories.

We eventually reached Year IV and it was campus time. This was the time when the companies visited the campus to offer us jobs. Where Virdi managed to make stories in the most ordinary settings, it was quite likely that he would make one if not some when the companies were visiting the campus. Virdi—a sardar that he was—had been seen in Rourkela only in his small turban. But keen to look a complete Sardar in his TISCO interview, he put on the big turban that day. His question to the college boys around before the interview was: "*Mein Sardar dikh raha hoon na* (Tell me if I am looking a Sardar)?" As it came from Virdi after his interview, the panel asked him a question about 'car battery' to which Virdi could not answer. He justified not knowing the answer to the fact that his father did not own a car. To this, the panel objected and one member maintained that one did not have to own a tool or a machine to know everything about it. "For instance," he said, "I do not have a generator at home, but you may ask me anything about it and I will answer." Virdi shot back. "What is there in a generator; even I know everything about generators." Virdi made it through the TISCO interview that day and it didn't matter what opinions his friends held about him being a complete Sardar; the panel was convinced he was one!

Once Virdi got his job, he decided to expand his horizons. For up until then he had kept himself away from any and everything that could come in the way of his studies. This included emotions and feelings that he realized he had kept suppressed. One such— and this was bound to come fizzing out once TISCO handed over the 'opener' to him in the form of a job— was his feeling towards Jhinki. Jhinki (this was her pet name) happened to be from a junior batch and now that Virdi had a job—boys were made to believe that having a job in hand gave them the license to apply the 'opener' to open their hearts out—Virdi considered taking the story to the next level. Interestingly, in the Boys Hostel, when a boy was known to have decided to speak his heart out to a girl, activities would be seen on the rise around his room. Many would be interested in knowing the progress; many others would show to be the well-wisher who could volunteer for any work that made the job easier for the Romeo. The boys would also help to strategize on the time, location and how-to-propose aspects of the project. In all, they would make sure that the project did not end midway!

Thanks to these well-wishers, Virdi was well on course. He came to know that Jhinki had enrolled in a software training course outside the college campus from where she would return around noon, every Saturday and Sunday. Came Saturday and Virdi planned to be at the college front gate around 11:45 in the morning with his batchmate Chitta who knew Jhinki. The idea was that Chitta would introduce Virdi to Jhinki and from where Virdi would take Jhinki by storm: "Virdi; *naam to suna hi hoga* (I am Virdi, you would have heard my name for sure)." Virdi could do that but only in his thoughts. Even before the tower clock could strike 12, Virdi gave up on his plans. "*Mere se nahi bunn parega, chal wapas hostel chalte hain* (I won't be able to do it. Let us return to the hostel)." Chitta kept motivating Virdi to not give up, up until the time he knew it was not working and at which time he felt like kicking Virdi's back with full throttle. Chitta's frustration stemmed from the fact that his effort involving escorting Virdi on such dazzling and scorching summer noon went completely futile. Worse still, what could have made an interesting story for the hostel boys that evening, was not to be.

The two rode their bicycles back to the hostel. As though "Deflated, Exhausted and Flogged" (**DEF**)!

After a lot of cajoling on part of Virdi, Chitta agreed to escort Virdi to ground zero the following day. On one condition though: if Virdi repeated the **DEF** on Sunday, Chitta would make it DEF**G** (**G** when declared in anger can be anybody's guess!). "It was Sunday and Jhinki would once again pass by that place by noon," was the calculation. And Virdi put on a brave face, convincing himself and more so Chitta that he would not disappoint "today". It was 11:45 in the morning and the two were seen having taken their positions on the ground!

20 minutes later

Virdi was riding the bicycle back to the hostel, all alone. What was peculiar about the ride was that Virdi, though riding at very ordinary speed, was seen standing while applying the pedals. It so happened that Virdi ended up repeating the DEF and Chitta made sure that he delivered the DEF(**G**) as promised! Virdi couldn't muster enough courage to speak his heart out to Jhinki. Sadly, his love story, like most other love stories of REC Rourkela, ended incomplete!

To Moon, by Train

Who doesn't like holidays, especially the unexpected ones? Ask your kids about the COVID bandh. We had a similar scenario in the year when our college management declared sine-die after the students took to the streets to protest reservations in government jobs. The college management had succeeded in foiling as many as two prior attempts on part of the students. Not the third. The students had been persistent and their efforts paid off!

The hostel jubilation, however, was short-lived. Mainly because we had to vacate the hostel at very short notice and rush to the nearest railway stations to book our tickets (remember we had no mobile and internet). And why was there no option to stay put in the hostel? Because in situations like this, the college would shut after police intervention. And the very reason for the *jinde-die* would be to disassemble the boys to prevent processions and bandhs!

I had a reasonable sense of the *unadulterated misadventure* for me in the coming days. To understand my predicament, you need to know that my parents were settled in Kohima and traveling from Rourkela to Kohima was almost like singing *Saat samundar par main tere/Peeche-Peeche aa gayi*. Rourkela to Kohima isn't seven seas apart but the mix of the ice-water-steam route from the source to the destination makes it a 14-seas-apart equivalent!

The journey begins with a train ride from Rourkela to Howrah followed by another from Howrah to Guwahati. The third train ride would take you only as far as Dimapur. And then comes the final leg of the journey—a bus ride to your final destination, Kohima! What is not implicitly evident in this four-leg journey is the interruption after every leg—just about every. For instance, your third leg may begin a good 12 or even 16 hours after your second leg ended. And this is because of the very few trains running in these routes. And even those said to be *running* are at most *limping*! It was the 1st of March when my journey began. I reached Howrah the following morning only to discover that out of the two daily Howrah-Guwahati trains, the first had already left. As though 'already left' were not enough, I came to know that the train had 'just left'. And the second, slated to leave late in the evening, stood canceled for the day! What that meant was that close to 24 hours after the college sent us packing, I had completed no more than 10% of my overall journey. What that also meant was that this status quo would show no change for the next 24 hours!

It was no surprise that I lost all patience and boarded the third train, the one that would take me back to Rourkela! It was already March 3rd when I reached Rourkela. When I reached the hostel, I couldn't hear even dogs barking. It was that deafening of a silence! I had the ghostly air of the hostel corridors whispering that I should not stay in the hostel. Two days after having called home to tell my mom that her *Raja beta* was on his way home to Kohima, I had to call home again. This time to tell her how some evil played black magic on my plans to reach Kohima!

My mom broke down on the phone and this was just the trigger I needed to attempt yet another train ride to Howrah, to reach Kohima. Unsure, I picked my bag—the same packed bag—and took the next train to Howrah. In all, March 1st saw me taking off from Rourkela. March 2nd saw me reach Howrah. March 2nd also saw me take the Rourkela-bound train. And it was Mar 3rd when I reached back to square one: Rourkela. The first launch having failed, it was time to attempt another launch!

Finally, as I was sitting on the train that would take me to Guwahati (on March 4th) I had an epiphany that this was the same train that had completed a round trip from Howrah to Guwahati and back that I had missed by a whisker a couple of days ago! To make up for the miss that day on March 2nd, it looked like Indian Railways had made special arrangements only for me. On this day, March 4th, the train was delayed by six hours. When the entire universe is conspiring against you, you do nothing except stay calm. I could so very easily identify the roots of my calmness in the Howrah-Guwahati train journey!

What gets *interesting*—and *interesting* because the word *frustrating would be undermining my condition*—is that a train delayed by six hours right at start generally adds as many hours till it reaches its destination. This train was no exception. Not sure if it was on the rails but struggling for sure, the train reached Guwahati station on March 5th a good 12 hours later than its scheduled time! Even the generally slow ticking station clocks at the Guwahati railway station indicated it was nine o'clock in the night. It was now my turn to inquire about the next train to Dimapur. The Train Inquiry Counter had the most devastating news for me: The next train to Dimapur was in the morning, a good 12 hours later! Buses ply in that route but not after six o'clock in the evening and that meant the next 12 hours of life would see me stranded in Guwahati.

Rourkela and Howrah get fairly warm by the first week of March; but not North-East India. But the mix of excitement and stupidity kept me unmindful of this fact when I left Rourkela. The result was that except for a pair of jeans and tees in my bag and an attempted funky short sleeve shirt I was on with, I carried nothing more. It was getting late in the night and Guwahati station was just beginning to get colder. I wrapped myself around with any and everything that I could find in my bag. On went my towel (the thin one, called g*amcha*) around my ears to make up for the absence of muffler. On I pulled my spare jeans up until where it could be pulled on top of another that I was already on with. And slowly but surely, I found that except for my pairs of spare inners, there was nothing left in my by-now near-empty airbag!

The next morning (March 6th), hoping that no trains were canceled nor delayed, it was now the penultimate leg of the seemingly never-ending journey. The train to Dimapur took off from Guwahati but never showed any signs of hurriedness on its part. I was not very far from what would be a week from the time the college management gifted us with the *break*. But I was defiantly far from where I had set out to be. If the Howrah-Guwahati train was the snail of my journey, this train could beat a sloth in being lazy. And finally, when the train arrived in Dimapur late in the evening on March 6th, it was once more a replay of the Guwahati story the previous evening. No cabs or buses run in the Dimapur-Kohima route after six o'clock in the evening and this meant my towel would make up for the absence of muffler the second night in a row as

I spent yet another night on the Railway Station, this time, Dimapur's!

I reached Kohima on the 7th of March precisely in one week. Remember, my first attempt to travel to Kohima (from Rourkela) was on Mar 1st. And this meant that if my *return* journey was as eventful as the earlier one, I would be in Rourkela no earlier than Mar 14th if I decided to return on the very day I reached Kohima! But my return journey is another story for another time (In the next chapter – **From Moon, by Train**).

From Moon, by Train

It often happens on reaching home from college after a long time that our parents inadvertently ask us, "*Beta, wapas kab jaana hai* (When are you bound to return)?" Even though I had thought a lot about this, I didn't have any conclusive answer. The reason being that this holiday was unplanned and unscheduled, given to us by political and divine intervention. Things became even more complicated because I couldn't connect to college easily. You need to remember that this was the era of no mobiles or internet and consequently, no college website.

The only option that suited me (but not my pocket) was to inquire by landline phone. A few attempts to call the college office got me severe pocket burns. This was because I had to call during the daytime and the maximum-distance STD charges for daytime calling were exorbitantly high during those days. A call would go unanswered and yet the phone meter would start ticking. Ouch!

When theories and logic do not work, we engineers resort to the *empirical* route. The previous trends had been fairly consistent: the hostel boys would take to the Rourkela streets to protest the government's order on reservations in government jobs. This would lead to police intervention. The college management, fearing violence, would then be left with no option but to declare the college closed. And the college would resume more or less a month after it closed. Going by the trend, I had all reasons to believe that the college would reopen about a month after it closed. This meant that two weeks after I reached Kohima (three weeks of college shutdown), it was time to consider returning. I was also expecting some surprises going by my track record of traveling.

In those days, Kohima did not show on the railway map. One had to travel all the way to Dimapur not only to start a train journey but also to book train reservations. Even though Kohima-Dimapur distance was not much, the route was time taking and very tiring. Looking at the pros and cons and left with no choice, I decided to try my luck once again and travel without reservations. Hmpf!

So after saying *phir-milenge* (see you again) to my parents, I took a bus to Dimapur and completed the first leg of my return journey uneventfully. I did thank my stars when the next leg, the Dimapur-Guwahati train trip too, ended without much of a hitch. First, the Kohima-Dimapur bus ride and then the Dimapur-Guwahati train journey had been uneventful, thankfully, but had left me exhausted. To think about the next leg—the Guwahati-Howrah train ride, without reservations—was unimaginable though. For two reasons: first, this route is a good four-times longer than Dimapur-Guwahati and second, it was around the last week of March and this meant that the rising temperature—which was not a concern while traveling to Kohima—was another hostility I had to be at the receiving end of. In those days, A/C coaches were for the elite class, not for us students!

I made a fruitless attempt to buy a reservation at the reservation counter only to satisfy myself and say that I tried. Interestingly though, Guwahati railway station offered alternatives! In those days you would find several spy-like boys and men at the Guwahati railway station looking out for people like me who needed to buy train reservations. Those like me desperate for a train reservation wore a smell that these boys and men could sniff and who they would approach. All in all, everyone has seen **chai-walas** at railway stations selling *chai*. At the Guwahati railway station, one also got to see **ticket-walas** selling train tickets!

These spies carried tickets of several routes; across genders and ages. They expertly carried tickets of many shapes and sizes tucked in some or other pockets to make sure they escaped the police radar. One boy aged around 16, after negotiating brilliantly for a price, showed me a ticket suiting my requirement. I would now travel to Howrah as Mr. Vijay, 26 years The only parameter that showed right on this ticket was 'M' (male), besides of course the train name and the date of journey. All in all, the ticket wasn't fake. I made it one by traveling on it!

My infant mustache and beard would have been enough to get me penalized. Therefore, I tried bearing a more mature look on myself during my train journey from Guwahati to Howrah in a conscious attempt to prove to the world that yes, I was indeed Vijay, a '26-year-old' mature 'male'.

It turned out that my Oscar-worthy acting was uncalled for as no one bothered to care. The train reached its final destination Howrah, and all passengers after disembarking were walking in the same direction. Some of these passengers whose final destination was Howrah would walk out of the station and many others like me, the transit passengers, would change platforms to catch the next train. And just when I was pretty sure that I was done and had dodged the shabby system that couldn't even make out that I was only 18 and not 26, came the TTE (Train Ticket Examiner), directing me to stand sideways, away from the stream in which the passengers were flowing.

The tall man was chewing tobacco and had his mouth full and this was an added reason why he was talking in sign language. From his expression and body language, it was evident that he had no doubt about me or the ticket or both being fake. Signaling to me to show the ticket—his mouth was fuller now and because of which his head was tilting further up as he uttered a word or two—he waited for me to follow his marching order: "show me your ticket."

I knew that the ticket was in my back pocket and yet kept searching around in my wallet to start with, then the bag and a few other places, buying time, to give myself ample time to have some thought cross me that could come to my rescue. Not to be! Many thoughts crossed, but none were worth executing. I considered telling him that I had lost my ticket. But very soon realizing that this excuse would not take me far, I decided to hand over the ticket to him. By then he could no longer hold his mouthful paan content and *pichhh* went the spit shoot! "Where did you buy this ticket from?" came his question and instead of telling him that I got it from a genuine railway reservation counter—which I would perhaps have done if I had indeed done—I pretended as though I did not even understand his question. By putting in that extra effort to show innocence, I wanted to prove that someone like me didn't even know where else to buy railway reservations from. The question came one more time and this time my answer was, "Railway Reservation Counter."

He looked seasoned for if he were not, he would have possibly got annoyed at my delayed responses.

Still chewing the leftover beetles in his mouth and remaining casual, he declared that my train journey had ended for the day and possibly for the year or two to follow because offenses of this category were grouped under section 420 of the Indian Penal Code (IPC). In short, this was a ripe case of cheat and fraud. He added further, with no tinge of assertion nor aggression whatsoever, that the crime came packaged with **three years in prison** and a penalty of up to **Rs. 3000**.

The thought crossed my mind that I had traveled to Kohima about three weeks ago because the college had declared sine-die following the hostel students taking to the Rourkela streets to protest a government decision. My participation then may not have been voluntary and was instead forced by the college seniors. But there was no denying that I had participated in the protest march and therefore, could so easily have been accused of instigating violence. And now, three weeks later, it was turning out that I had completed all groundwork for being charged with *Cheat* and *Deceit* under **IPC Section 420**. What this was if not the gala launch of a modern-day political career!

Between the two of us, one had to break the ice about the possible workaround. There was only one workaround: **bribing him to let me go!** But if I were to propose that, I feared that he would tell me about added subsections of IPC section 420 that I might be charged under - *cheat, deceit* and **bribery**! And then, besides 'protest marches' and 'fake tickets', my resume would also show 'attempting to bribe'. **Result**: three years behind bars could just sound revised as much as the Rs. 3,000 penalty would! And that could mean, slowly but surely, I would be on course to indeed becoming M 26 by the time my jail term ended! I held on, totally unsure about how life in jail would be. I was also beginning to accept that *Rahu-Ketu* had a distinctive role to play in the lives of humans and that the March month of that year had a terrible planetary misalignment in my disfavor. All these thoughts were queuing up in my mind when the TTE broke the ice. "Ok, how much can you pay?" was how he started.

Hurrying to locate and pick all cash I had from the nooks and corners of my pockets and my wallets and my bag pockets and just about everywhere, I gave him all. My hurriedness stemmed from the fact that there was one, just one opportunity for me to avert a historic downfall. So, even before the TTE possibly changed his mind and reverted to his honest ways, I decided to set myself free from the catastrophe hovering over me! The TTE continued to wear that calm and composed look on his face as he walked away with my last penny, pretending to imply that he usually was very strict and honest, but that he bent his ways that day only to do me a favor!

As though the misaligned stars had just decided to ease further in my favor, I recalled that 100-rupee note that the Guwahati ticket-wala had returned to me after much bargaining and negotiation and which

I happened to put aside in my shirt pocket. The reason I missed emptying this pocket unlike every other into the TTE's was that I seldom kept anything in my shirt pocket and had totally forgotten having kept this 100-rupee note there.

After buying the Howrah-Rourkela train ticket, I had just enough pennies left to buy peeled peanuts (*mumfali*). Continuing the last leg of my journey from Howrah to Rourkela hungrier and beaten, I couldn't help thanking and blessing a very honest TTE who bent his ways to rescue me! Had he not discounted that day and remained 'firm and honest' as he 'supposedly' was every other day, I would still have been traveling but to Howrah Jail!

Aaj Se Main Tumhe Banti Bulaungi

What is in a name? Well, just about everything. Of the many identities one may have, a *name* stands right up there. Interestingly, many a time, men perceive someone's integrity, individuality, nature, culture, confidence and much more by names. They become oblivious to the fact that one does not undergo an apprenticeship to be awarded a name. It comes to one right after birth and at times even before it, but the world's expectations about a man are often driven by names. *Naam Sushil aur kaam Jalil; Naam Bade aur Darshan Chotte* and many more phrases, idioms and similes are characteristics of the variances between expectations and realities!

Other than names at birth (first name) and names by birth (surnames), consistency in actions also qualifies people for additional titles and names. From *Mahatma Gandhi* to *Lokmanya Tilak*, from *Missile Man* to *Master Dluster*, the world has been conferring titles and names to humans since times immemorial. But while there are titles that have made women and men proud, there are others that have been pasted upon them without caring about their consent. Not just consistency, at times factors well beyond you determine your name or title. I know of a **Sa**chin **Pat**il who was called **Sapat**! My REC Rourkela 2nd year roomie Shant Patel hailed from Porbandar (Gujarat) and that was all required of him to be named **Bapu**! The name fitted Shant like a second skin. No wonder he came to Rourkela a 'Shant'; he left Rourkela a 'Bapu'! But for his *give everything a damn* attitude, Ashish Saxena would not have been a **Raja Babu**. Chubby cheeks did not justify the name Rajneesh as much as **Golu** did. Deependra had grey hair and he was the **Uncle** of the batch!

The *naamkaran* (nicknaming) got to people on the campus beyond the students. The hostel canteen chai *wala* had the origin of his name in his semblance to the yesteryear Bollywood actor **Keshto Mukherjee**. This naming (Keshto) had been administered long before we reached Rourkela and hardly anyone knew that he was not Keshto in real! The lone medical doctor on the campus—to be seen in the college dispensary in the evening hours administering the same pills whether you had a headache or fever—

was Dr. Jhatka. This name had its origin in the once-famous cartoon character.

Prof. Jamuna Prasad was named 'write fast' because he would always be in a hurry while dictating notes. "Write fast, I have to finish the course" was his trademark line that we would get to hear no fewer than five times in any and every class. The lady professor teaching us **Dynamics** in Engineering Mechanics was **Buri** only because her counterpart teaching us **Statics** in Engineering Mechanics was Prof. (Mr.) **Bura**! The re-identification was confined not just to bizarre naming but beyond. When our Electrical batch visited a substation as part of a study tour, the professor accompanying us (Prof. Sahoo) asked the batch about the humming sound heard around substations. Ritesh, in a soft voice, obviously to ensure that his voice did not reach Prof. Sahoo, stated that Prof. Mohanty was sitting inside! Prof. Mohanty was an Asst. Professor in the Electrical Department with a slight stammer in speech when he began speaking. His stuttering would subside after he went past the first word in his speech but until then, his sound would resemble the hum generated by the transformer!

CalC for 'calculator', *Lag Gayi* for 'I am screwed', *Baap* for 'immediate senior in the same branch from the same state (province)'; these were some other commonly used terms and phrases. These had become an intrinsic part of the hostel lexicon over the years. Anupam declared that his *baap* had come from

Shillong and was not amused to see the ashtray in his hostel room. Anupam hailed from Shillong and was referring to his biological dad who 'recently' visited him in Rourkela. Khati had two questions. Which 'Shillong *wala baap*' was he referring to and why would a *baap* (senior) not be amused to see an ashtray in a hostel room where every Tom, Dick and Harry smoked!

Some terms were way more versatile and their meanings could only be deciphered from the context in which those were used. **Item** was one such term. *Mere saath **item** ho gaya* meant I was at the receiving end of something ridiculous. But when someone said *1ˢᵗ year Electrical mein ek **item** aayi hei*, it would mean a beautiful girl had joined the 1ˢᵗ year Electrical batch. Excitingly, this term used in the context of boys usually meant funny or absurd. *Gaurav **item** hei* for instance would mean 'Gaurav is silly!'

That was the hostel world where the air abounded with nicknames waiting to be conferred. At times it could be your passion that would get you one; at other times it had to be your day and nothing more. For instance, our senior Sarangi scored a 50 in a Cricket match with the seniors when he was in his first year. And that was all he had to do to be conferred the title **Captain.** Seniors and juniors alike, everyone called him 'captain' up until he completed his Engineering inning four years later. As though that were not enough, close to 30 years after that knock, he remains a **Captain!**

Tu Kaan Pakad... Aur Tu... Chal Naanch...

College...First Days...

It was a price to pay for getting enrolled into the league of grown-ups. So many people around but there were none whom I knew. This was in stark contrast to the life in Kohima up until the previous week where there was not a place in the entire town where a look around would not show me a familiar face. It was so very easily the change that every other change combined across the 18 years preceding it could not match. In the REC Rourkela Hostel, none cared if I did not like the breakfast; none bothered if I was considering skipping my day's lunch.

My first day on the campus happened to be a fortnight before my first day in the hostel. I was on the campus to complete my admission formalities and my dad had accompanied me to make sure I did not miss out on filling the forms appropriately which otherwise '*could well cost me the college seat!*' 101 forms to fill, together with 201 interruptions by the 2nd year boys gave good indications of how life in REC Rourkela was going to be.

"*Kaun sa branch hei be G*n*du* (what's your branch a**h**le)?"I would hear from a boy around. His tone, expression and body language got me to momentarily forget my branch. Not sure if I was supposed to respond with a smile or without, I tried to tread the middle path. "*Electrical,*" I said. And at this, he gave a loud shout to a couple more 2nd year boys around that were busy outsmarting other 101-form fillers. On hearing my branch, they rushed towards me to let me know that I was 'finished'! Their expression read '*empathy with scare*'. For a moment, I would be forced into believing that Electrical Engineering in REC Rourkela was most likely about being subjected to high voltage electric shocks! "*What is Ohm's law?*" And I read it out with some relief that I did not draw a blank. But very soon the questions got the better of me, so much that I was on the brink of losing out on the unit of electric current!

We would soon go on to discover that the guys who asked the most questions pretending they were reincarnations of Benjamin Franklin, were the most struggling Electrical Boys in Year II. And very soon, into semester I, we would go on to know who those quizzers from my batch would be when the freshers made their way into the college the following year!

It was the first day in college when our classes began and most of the 1st year boys were in new outfits. Well-creased trousers and shirts that we had just got stitched a week prior (readymade pants were still not common those days) with shoes that had not stopped hurting yet; the dress-up was as fresh. It took very little time to discover though that anything that would make you noticeable—dress or shoes, physique or tantrums, stubbles or baldness—was to be shed for the coming few months, or else...

Hostel I was where we 1st year boys resided. At the end of day 1 in college, there were already two groups in the hostel. One that had received the vaccine shots (thrashes) from the senior boys and the others who knew that their share was coming. And the ones who received the shots (beatings) were an aggrieved lot. Not because their pains had not subsided but because they were not issued any immunization certificate. And this meant they had no guarantee that they won't receive more! All in all, life looked terrible and with the 1st year boys not allowed to switch on lights at nights, it was all about 'crying in the dark!' Oh, what a fall from the pampered times just a week ago when I would not bother to turn the lights off even when I slept off; mom would take care!

Hostel I had four-seater rooms and good sense had prevailed over the college management that year. This hostel was kept reserved only for the 1st year students.

The pious initiative notwithstanding, senior boys would often sneak in and run havoc in the hostel. Now and then some senior boys would enter the hostel, run the vaccine doses on as many boys they pleased; spill out some filthy words and shout out expletives that we 1st year boys would wish we weren't alive to lend ears to. These apparent hooligans were 2nd year boys 95% of the time and it was unfathomable in our view how one year of Rourkela hostel/college stay could bring such sea change in language, tone and living ways in the boys. It seemed implausible that we would transform even 10%. But then they say, *seeing is believing*. We would go on to see and believe how in one year, we were as much transformed!

The *senior aa gaya* alert would echo in Hostel I now and then as though *tiger aa gaya*. And we kittens would run places to avert vaccination shots. At midnight a group of no more than two to three 2nd year boys would be enough to cause turmoil in Hostel I, making us all brush our teeth. At other times we would be asked to make a train of uncovered bogeys (don't tell me you don't get this) and there we would be, holding the connectors and running around the hostel singing **chhoook-chhoook** in chorus! **Pranav**, **Saiket** and **Sanjay** had bubble-sorted themselves to fame as singers and would often be heard obliging to the seniors' choices for songs. Interestingly, we were expected to be in formals 24*7 and that meant even toilet visits (there were no western-style commodes) were all in trousers. You could remove your shoes if you pleased once you latched yourself in! If Shashi Tharoor were to present this story, it would make the most unbelievable read whereby the hostel would be likened to the most stylish and formal in the history of mankind where even the toilet visits were in formals!

Long days and longer nights made the 24 hours in a day. We would walk to the college at seven-thirty in the morning. The half-a-km walk was filled with unending variants of rascality on part of the senior boys. The seniors walking alongside the queue of 1st year boys—yes, every morning, we were supposed to walk in a queue from the hostel to college— seemed like the shepherds steering the livestock to the grasslands, flashing the crook (stick) now and then. And the similarities did not end there. We were required to keep our eyes on our third shirt button (from the top) to compensate for the masks that we were not required to wear, unlike the grazers!

As though the rowdiness in the hostel was not enough, many a time the senior boys would enter our classrooms, intermittently between classes when the professor was not around. Aimed more at getting a closer view of the 1st year girls, these boys, while in the class, expended extra efforts at being smart. Their calculation was based on the presumption—strangely rogue and childish—that with the 1st year boys running for cover, they (the seniors) had a start in the race when it came to hooking the girls! The fact that the girls to boys ratio in the college was astoundingly low, 99% of the senior boys were still nomadic and what they thought would stamp their impression among the 1st year girls, exposed their desperation instead!

From July until the end of December, nothing would change. The grassland grazing would continue; the vaccination shots would keep improving our immunity to the extent that by the end of December, we would see for ourselves how near 100% transformed we were. We could make out how badly we were waiting for the 1st year boys (and girls) to arrive in the college in another six to seven months when we would call out our classmates aloud to let them know that *this boy* belonged to the Electrical branch. "You are 'finished'" would be our declaration. And it would be 'fun', we would believe, to experience how 'finished' he felt at this announcement!

Typhoid in the Hostel and the Cozy Hospital

'The end of the ragging period would mark the victory of non-violence over violence,' or so would the 1st year hostel boys believe. They wanted to be optimistic that gone would be the days when senior boys would thrash anyone in the 1st year batch. The Hostel I— this was where the first years dwelled—was waiting for the Aug 15, 1947 moment in their hostel. The day came, but just as there was partition bloodshed in the aftermath of Indian Independence, the freedom celebration in the hostel too was short-lived. There was a Typhoid outbreak and the boys started rushing to IG Hospital, the lone reasonable hospital in Rourkela during those days.

Freshwater supply in the hostel lasted mere 30–45 minutes every morning and this was the time when the hostel boys could take baths. If you missed the water supply bus on a day—and just about every day many did—the next bath stop would be a day away! The hostel was divided into quite some blocks and each hostel block had a bathroom count of six, one among which was bricked at its door up to the waist height. Along with the walls on the other sides, this was the water storage for the larger of nature's calls.

It was against the spirit of hostel empowerment to have this tank cleaned. Ever! Even the so-called fresh water supply had significant mineral content besides mud. A handful of water would appear yellow or orange. It is said that many bacteria forms breach the immune system of a human only once. Human bodies generate enough antibodies thereafter. So much so that the same bacteria forms cannot rip you again. By ensuring near-zero water care systems in the hostel, the hostel management judiciously believed that the hostel dwellers would generate these antibodies aplenty. This belief conveyed empowerment: Go, fight the devil in bacteria and all micro-organisms all yourselves; hang on till they succumb!

The college and the hostel management wore a fair semblance to the age-old Zamindari system where the field workers were pretty much held hostage by the zamindars[4]. Time had changed and the zamindari system might have long gone, but what did not change in the college and the hostel was the underlying essence of that coercion. Students questioning the system were looked down upon by the management as traitors. But sensing the rate at which the hostel rooms were getting locked out (many rooms had the entire gang of four admitted into IG Hospital), the hostel boys decided to bell the cat. We went to the hostel warden to let him know that it was better to be tagged traitors than martyrs. Because slowly but surely, the two tags were getting mutually exclusive! The warden, Prof. Damodar, lent a patient ear to us and assured us that he was on course to get the best possible solution in the hostel at the earliest that would free the hostel water of all maladies.

Hopeful, the boys decided to withstand the bacterial onslaught for a day or two more until Prof. Damodar came right on his assurances. Very soon, Prof. Damodar came back with the result of the lab findings where the hostel water sample had apparently been sent for testing. Students were excited. But when the hostel superintendent declared the result, everyone was in shock, scratching their heads. As

---

4 Under the Zamindari system, the zamindars were recognized as owners of the lands. Zamindars were given the right to collect the rent from the peasants and the system was discriminatory in that the peasants had no say whatsoever over the rulings and ruthlessness of the zamindars.

per Prof. Damodar, the lab found the water quality to be great on all counts. Students had a valid reason to doubt the results of the lab findings. When senior management does not pay heed to your prayers and requests, it gets sickening. But when it starts lying too, it gets puking! With regard to the water sample testing good and healthy, we hostel boys could list down a few possibilities in the increasing order of likelihood:

- The lab apparatuses were no better than the hostel water sample

- The lab was run on the Gandhian principle that advocated looking for the good in a person, place, or thing as all in that person, place, or thing and never looking for any bad. That way, the test found nothing bad with the water sample!

- The lab team was lying

- No such labs existed in the town

- No water was ever sent to any lab

All in all, the hostel stay was not only about diseases and living with lies, but also about accepting life as it came. The boys were also getting used to the realities of life that would teach them patience and to live life, come what may. The entire episode got the boys to appreciate and accept one philosophy more than any other: '*Samey se pehle aur Bhagya se adhik, kisi ko kuch nahi milta hei* (You don't get before your time comes and beyond what your fate has for you).' In short, the writing was on the wall: 'Accept the lab verdict, and thank Prof. Damodar for keeping up on his promises!'

Meanwhile, the Hostel I population was dwindling by the day; moving to the IG Hospital. They say, "In times of war, make peace." The boys, irrespective of all differences and rivalries just in case, were helping one another out. From arranging meals for the ailing to escorting a needy to the hospital, the boys exhibited great fellowship. Since many in the punctured lot now admitted in the hospital needed blood, the boys who were hale and healthy came forward to donate blood. It was in this stream that Sanjeev complained of fever and body ache. And in came Nageswar to accompany Sanjeev to the hospital. Nageswar took a step further in being the male Mother Teresa of all times by volunteering to donate blood at the hospital. As Sanjeev underwent a few routine checks, Nageswar's blood sample was examined as part of the hospital procedure to ensure that the blood donated in the hospital blood bank was free from any irregularities. The results were out and while Sanjeev's ailment was found out to be minor following which he returned to the hostel, Nageswar's blood sample tested positive for Typhoid. Mother Teresa had to be admitted to the hospital!

Meanwhile, the IG Hospital was getting cozier. A young nurse attending on Nikhil was willing to take nursing to the next level. She suggested that Nikhil allowed her to sleep on the same bed as him, for then, she would just be a breath away from him as against 'a call or a shout away' that was coming in the way of quick assistance and nursing. Nikhil was shocked. He was aware '*Do jawan ladka/ladki kabhi dost nahi ho sakte* (A young boy and a young girl can never be friends).' Good or bad for Nikhil or the nurse, somehow Nikhil summoned the courage to convince the nurse that it was not possible. If the typhoid outbreak had happened in one of the later years by which time Nikhil had developed significant antibodies, a similar proposal from the nurse to Nikhil would definitely have met a different fate!

In the meantime, the hostel management was rolling out safety measures in the hostel way beyond assurances and promises! Having got the water sample tested fit for drinking on all counts, the management now got a water boiler installed in the hostel. The idea was to have boiled drinking water filled in a tank which the boys would then fill their flasks or bottles from. Great idea but imagine 350 students awaiting turns to fill their water bottles from one outlet!

To improve the efficiency, someone came up with a Nobel prize-winning idea to just open the lid at the top, so that everyone could fill their water bottle from the top. But as soon as they opened the lid of the tank, students saw a big dead cockroach floating. Everyone was in shock but Ravi evoked thoughts deeper than the Pacific Ocean. He said "*Tabhi tau mai bolun, ye paani aaj itna meetha kyon lag raha. Aaj ke pehle tau kabhi nahi laga* (I was wondering why the water tasted so sweet today. Never felt that before)."

From the Nageshwars to the Nikhils, the boys, stronger than ever with an army of antibodies within them, started returning to the hostel. Prof. Damodar was relieved that one more year passed by without martyrdom and that the next water sample test was now at least a year away when the next batch started rushing to the IG Hospital!

I Will Get a Girlfriend for Sure

Story of Year I: Started with a Flicker; ended with a Flash

311 boys; 19 girls. This wasn't the number at a small-town prison. It was instead the count of our batch of Rourkela RENGCOLIANS. It was only obvious that the queue of boys at every window—damn every 19—was ridiculously long where a queuer

did not have to have *promises to keep,* but definitely had *miles to go before he made it there!* The only other queues that could match the RENGLOLIAN boys' across all counts—length, vigor, intensity, hope, and despair—were the ATM queues post 2016 demonetization!

With the competition at the windows being cut-throat, strategizing on the approach to come up with *winning moves* was a necessity, not just a volition. Very soon, everyone in the Boys Hostel, well almost everyone, was convinced that what mattered the most was that the girl held an impression about him; it mattered little if the impression was *good* or *bad.* The overall idea was to get into the bus somehow, anyhow; for only then would he stand a chance of getting a seat! And this was the first of the many strategies that the Rourkela stay would unfold.

How she smiled at me when I greeted her... How that scoundrel was trying to impress her stupidly... How that guy—another rascal just because he belonged to the same queue—made a fool of himself in the class and will now find it impossible to recover the lost ground... How every such past fascination with girls was merely infatuation and how this one is 'true love'... How I considered an achievement in itself at being teased in the name of some girl... Overall, the Boys Hostel was fast turning into that world where the Kishore Kumar fans were rising by the day. From *Yeh Shaam Mastani* and *Mere Sapno ki Rani* to *Mera Jeevan Kora Kagaz* and *Ghongroo ki tarah,* there was a Kishore Kumar number that fitted everyone. The most prosaic of the boys were turning poets overnight. Overall, the Engineering hostel saw music and poetry abound, just about making up for the dust catching up on the course books!

Taking a step back, it wasn't as though the *Romeo Syndrome* had hit the boys right on day one of their Rourkela innings. Far from it, the first year—and particularly the first semester—was that time of the hostel stay when the boys missed home, the gully cricket they played with the colony boys, the bicycle ride down the countryside with school friends and much more. The first semester was that time when **Rahul** would still turn red, blushing, at recalling that accidental **Neha's** touch when the Plus-Two gang had been to a picnic towards the end of their school inning. The touch had got Rahul's heart racing with escape velocity, just refusing to slow down. The boys were growing up but had not grown enough to get past the most stupid of love lines: *True love is just once.* No wonder Rahul would allow only Neha and no one else in his dreams!

Many of these mama's boys up until a few weeks ago—just before they reached Rourkela—did not even bother dropping their soiled plates in the kitchen sink after meals; mama would take care. Most never had to expend thoughts on how and where their neatly ironed jeans came from. Not anymore. It was time instead to wash clothes on their own. It was time instead to discover how much a bar of Super Rin costs. Overall, the emotions ran high and any drop in its level just about any time was assuredly more than made up by the heavy downpour of slaps, hits, bangs and spanks from the college seniors as part of the **Ragging** Mahotsava! Overall, the first semester—*limping semester* would sound apter—went on just like that and the boys had no reprieve from the *murky, black ragging fog*, right till the end.

The wheel of time turned past the *limping semester* to take the boys past the Semester I fog. We were now in Semester II and the clearer sky gave ample indications of the *seasons changing*. And together with the seniors becoming friendlier, life in Rourkela seemed like the quivering sun, slowly but surely getting the better of the clouds. The boys were now uncaged unlike in the ragging days and could visit the eating joints around the campus beyond the hostel mess. They found out how cutting expenses on some items, branded toiletries for instance, could help them save just enough money to pay to the *dhobi* to get rid of the toil involving washing clothes. The Rahuls for the first time showed signs of weariness towards the Plus-Two **Nehas** in line with: *But she didn't have a heart, did she? For if she did, would she not have reciprocated my two-year-long fountains of gratitude with at least one drop of benevolence?* The college **Snehas** started to look more real and appealing, slowly but steadily on course to unseating the Plus-Two Nehas. To the boys, the distinct line *True love is just once* was just about getting blurrier, in line with: *But that (Neha) was just infatuation!* The east-facing windows—nearly all 19—untouched so far, were just about clinking, clanking and clattering to the Easterly now, reminding one and all that when seasons change, no one twig can remain impervious.

Thus the first year at RFC Rourkela ended. But not before showing the outlines and frames of the most mouth-stretching, tongue-tangling and lip-wrenching stories that the coming years were on course to unravel.

Year II: Started Calm;
Ended Windy

Kaddu ka Kamra

Elephants are mightily strong, strong enough to pull the wooden peg holding the chain that chains them. However, they are *conditioned* to believe that they cannot break the bonds of the chain. Human life too is about *conditioning*. A *chor* would risk his life while attempting to break into a high-security bank. A non-*chor* on the other hand would pass by a vault of jewelry (*khazana*) with no guard beside and yet notice nothing. In all, it is not about the physical locks, chains, or guards as much it is about the moral police within us.

Sumit Gupta (aka **Kaddu**) believed in this wisdom way more than anyone else in the hostel. He would lock his hostel room but would not carry the key along. He would instead place it at the top of the ventilator opening right above the door. This was an open secret to all in the hostel. *Why then did he lock when he was to place the key a mere foot or two away*? Because this, he thought, would get the hostel inmates to be aware that he was away when he was not around. *Why could he not carry the key with him?* Possible reasons ranged from *fear* to *superstition* and from *religious beliefs* to *omen*, but none could make out why. He would put off this question in jest. But all in all, anyone could walk into his room anytime, irrespective of whether Kaddu was in his room or far away!

Nishant, **Shalin** and **Prabhu** were at Keshto's for *chai*. Keshto ran the hostel canteen. Keshto's stocks included inexpensive merchandise to suit the affordability of the ever-cash-strapped hostel boys. **Tiger** biscuits sold for Rs.2 a pack and was a super hit among the hostel boys. There would be 10 biscuits in the pack and usually two boys, at times three, would share the cost. And this would get things fairly economical. With nine biscuits from the pack shared between the three, Nishant, Shalin and Prabhu were magnanimous enough to offer the 10th to one stray dog. Besides the hungry boys, the Keshto's arena also showed many hungrier dogs waiting for such showers of magnanimity when the 10th biscuit from the *Tiger* pack would go their way! Some trios were not as generous and would go on to divide the 10th one too into three!

The hungry dog (let's call it **Bruno**) was overwhelmed at the generosity. So much so that once the three were on their way back to the hostel, Bruno too followed them. Bruno was indebted beyond words. The three were indifferent to start with, but beyond a point their concern levels started to rise in wonderment as to when and until where would Bruno follow them in an apparent attempt to repay debts! The three reached the hostel and so did Bruno.

Nishant's hostel room was on the second floor and as he started climbing the stairs, Bruno followed. Nishant tried some soft techniques from some distance to dissuade him from following him any farther. He tried to express in some sign language (because Bruno could not follow Hindi, English, or Gujrati) that the 10th biscuit was a mere workaround to have the biscuit packet shared amongst three because 10 biscuits could not be divided amongst three! Nishant was a mix of frustration and helplessness when he had Bruno right beside him, all set to follow him into his room. Nishant was delaying opening his door. Just then a neighboring room that too was locked, caught Nishant's attention. Interestingly, even though this room was locked, Nishant had the magic key to unlock it. All he had to do was to rise on his heels, fetch the key that was placed over the ventilator opening above the door and open the lock. Yes, this neighboring room was Kaddu's!

This was the *light at the end of tunnel* moment for Nishant! His frustration made way for cheer. He opened the gateway to Kaddu's Empire and let Bruno in. Nishant now knew that he was just the final step away from getting rid of Bruno who had, albeit as a gesture of gratification, run amok through his mind. Making sure that he did not step into the room even when the door lay open, he let Bruno in. And no sooner was Bruno in than Nishant closed the door and locked it from outside. Alas! Bruno's moments of triumph happened to be so short-lived! What this was if not *destiny*!

What a betrayal for Bruno! Darkness descended upon him rendering him clueless about what life had in store. All this was the price Bruno was paying for one Tiger biscuit. At Rs.2 for 10, the one biscuit was worth 20p. And the reason why Bruno had got this 20p worth of 'shit' was that 10 is not a multiple of 3. Nothing more and nothing less. Bruno could be heard barking for a while. But not for long. After all, just because his intake was a 'Tiger' biscuit, it could not inject in him the power of the big cat!

It had been the longest hour of his life for Bruno when Kaddu—in an avatar of Lord Krishna that day—reached his room. After all, only Kaddu could set Bruno free. If Bruno had experienced the longest wait ever, Kaddu was all set to experience the greatest mix of mystery and surprise. And it all depended on how much strength Bruno was left with. If Bruno could still manage to keep himself strong with the 20p shit for hours and the greatest betrayal of his life, it could well be bad news for Kaddu. For then, Bruno would settle for nothing less than what it takes 14 sharp needles for a human to get the better of! Kaddu was singing aloud *Darwaza khula chod aayi / Nind ke maare* while unkeying the lock. The movie had released in and around that time and this song—more for the tone and the words—was a hit among the boys. Kaddu was oblivious to the fact that the next moment or two could well be his most decisive!

By now humming the song because he possibly did not know any more of the lyrics, Kaddu opened the door. And as he stepped inside, he heard the bark of his life! The bark seemed to be questioning Kaddu as to how on Earth could he (Kaddu) set foot inside the room! Bruno had by then made merry in the room. The soft pillow that Kaddu was so very fond of, lay on the ground and the cotton balls now free from the stitches, spanned quite some area on the floor. The creases on the bedsheet described how Bruno regarded everything in the room as his own. Bruno continued to bark loud at Kaddu to let him know that he (Bruno) was not liking his (Kaddu's) arrival one bit! Unsure about how to have Bruno taken off his room, Kaddu stood quiet. The *Darwaza khula chod aayai* hum had made way for a mute *Hanuman Chalisa* (Kaddu was a Hanuman bhakt!). And the confidence in Bruno's barks got Kaddu to take a step or two back. Nishant who had been overseeing the developments from some corner of the hostel corridor, stepped in, inquiring from Kaddu what made him still and mute. *"Bolta kyun nahi Kaddu? Kya hua?* (Why don't you speak up Kaddu? What's the matter?)," came the question from Nishant in apparent bewilderment and haze as though he would shoot the one responsible for Kaddu's stoic state! Nishant's excitement was conspicuous in his pretension. And why not? Nishant had of late started realizing that locking Bruno in Kaddu's *kamra* was not a great idea. And therefore, when he heard Bruno barking at Kaddu in excitement with all might, Nishant was relieved to know that Bruno had had the hour of his life in Kaddu's room. So much so that he (Bruno) was not ready to vacate!

The hostel boys led by Nishant got into the act of placating Bruno; letting Bruno know that he had the world to take refuge in unlike Kaddu who had none more than room no. 62. Nishant knew of Bruno's preferences. He advised Kaddu to quickly run and fetch a pack of Tiger biscuits from Keshto's. Bruno had his *Nag Panchmi* moment in the hostel that day. The boys offered him Tiger biscuits from the corridor outside Kaddu's door—this time 10 in number—and the shine in Bruno's eyes was palpable! Operation Bruno-*devta* concluded with Bruno having the last laugh!

Nishant, **Shalin** and **Prabhu** did not stop visiting the Keshto's. But they made sure they switched over to a packet of Krackjack thereafter. The pack sold for Rs.4 and was made up of 12 biscuits!

Masala Chai at Keshto

The one most known name and face at REC Rourkela, without doubt, was **Keshto's**. No one bothered to know his real name, for it never came to many minds that Keshto was his nickname. His looks wore a fair semblance to the yesteryear Bollywood actor and comedian **Keshto Mukherjee**. And for this reason, some noble soul—God knows who and how long ago—named him Keshto. So long ago, that in all likelihood even Keshto had forgotten his real name!

Keshto was the lone official *chai wala* in the Boys Hostel arena. No wonder, his canteen ran house-full no matter when, no matter what! To the boys in the hostel, "Keshto *challen*?" was that question phrase that came to the tips of their tongues when they were happy; when sad; when confused about what to do; when making up their mind to sit at the study table; when thoughtless. *Rich in water, poor in sugar and tea-dust* and *begging for milk*; Keshto's *chai* was lousy by any standards. The only parameter on which the boys had some say was 'hot tea'. Left to him, Keshto would draw a blank even on this count!

The official chai canteen in the hostel area had more to it: the *sutta* (cigarette). Goes without saying, *sutta* wasn't official canteen merchandise. But the fact that *chai* could only rejuvenate hearts; not souls, Keshto proved to be that agent of nature who made provisions for nourishing the souls too! Keshto's *sutta* stocks at the canteen comprised two variants: **without filter** costing a rupee per stick, and **with filter** costing 25 paise more. The 'filter cigarette was a marketing gimmick on part of the cigarette manufacturers way back in the 50s aimed at holding the cigarette addicts who were considering hanging their cigarette boots following the release of the first medical studies that linked smoking to lung cancer. The overall idea of 'filter cigarettes', as the manufacturers claimed, was that the filter screened out the *tar* and *nicotine* to make cigarettes safer. Where every penny counted, it was obvious that the hostel boys would not fall into any such marketing gimmicks whereby they paid extra just to make some poison less poisonous—well, just in case they ever considered cigarettes 'poisonous'! No wonder, the 'without filter variant sold the lion's share at Keshto's.

Coming to *chai* at Keshto, its quality, terrible that it was, had a lot to do with the paying patterns at Keshto's. Many boys would not pay. Sadly, Keshto did not have any recovery mechanisms. The most he could do and which he did profusely was to ensure that a cup of tea cost near to nothing to him so that if even merely half the hostel population paid their share, it would well make up for the remaining half. Interestingly, beverages including tea can still taste worse no matter how pathetic they have been, if the one preparing it decides to cut further on their cost. This has to be the case with most edibles. On select days, Keshto's *chai* would taste abysmally awful. When this happened, it was an easy guess that Keshto had to cut down further on its cost because a more sizeable hostel population—way beyond 50%—had defaulted on the payment the previous day!

On the whole, Keshto was soft on the hostel boys. And that explained how despite selling such low-quality *chai*, Keshto was liked. He was reasonably *soft-spoken* and consequently enjoyed the mass' goodwill. Another reason why the boys loved Keshto was his *simplicity*. And the third reason which stood way above the first two was his *generosity*. Interestingly, *generosity* was not what he opted for but what he had to accept for himself, for there was nothing much he could do when the boys did not pay! If Keshto could still survive and make a living for himself, it was because his **generosity** complemented his **expertise** in chai-making. One without the other would have so very easily ended his continuance in the campus!

One humor piece, rather satirical, associated with Keshto had to do with how he cared little about the boys paying (or not) for tea. And this had to do with the few levers he had in his hand for cutting down on its cost and consequently recovering the loss. This was unlike *suttas* where there was only a meager, fixed amount he could save on each stick with no recovery ways if the **solid** cigarette **turned** vapor (gas) without the **liquid** cash coming Keshto's way! This explained why Keshto would be extra vigilant when a sutta customer visited him. The *without-filter* variant was priced at ₹1 per stick, as much as a cup of *chai*. And the story goes thus: Having *sipped a cup of tea* and *puffed a sutta stick*, a boy—who now owed Keshto ₹2—realized that he had just ₹1 with him and no more. There was nothing that the boy or Keshto could do about it; the boy pleaded with Keshto to let him pay for the sutta at a later time. *"No way,"* was Keshto's reaction, for Keshto had no ways of recovering the losses on *sutta*. A mix of *angst, disappointment, frustration* and *helplessness* would envelop Keshto at any such episode when someone was not paying him for *sutta*. There was another proposal from the boy. *"Ok Keshto, this one rupee is for the sutta; I will pay for the chai later."* At having just averted the *sutta* loss, Keshto's face lit up! Made him a winner! Not just soft-spoken, simple and generous was Keshto; in his child-like innocence, he was godly too!

Keshto would also be pleased when a defaulter sounded honest. Hordes of boys dodged Keshto day in and night out when it came to the chai payment.

But some amongst them would be more noticeable to Keshto than others. When Keshto would insist on such boys to pay, not letting them go, the boys would come up with some advanced variant of fool-play, "*Keshto, I owed you ₹5 and together with the ₹1 now, I owe you ₹6. I will clear all payments when I come here tomorrow.*" Keshto liked such honest-sounding talks; a different matter that the boys would manufacture more honest-sounding fool-plays the next time they visited Keshto, to get away yet again!

Many years on, we recall how the Keshto's was such an inseparable and integral part of our Rourkela stay. Considering the number of batches that would have had similar experiences with him, many are and will always remain indebted to him. Not just because he was the lone *chai wala* in the hostel arena, but also for being gracious in accommodating all who needed to sip a cup of *chai*, irrespective of whether the sipper carried in his pocket a coin or a dodge!

Birthdays in the Boys Hostel

Some movie lines elicit **roars**; others, **vengeance**. Many from the villains reflect **glee** and those with **Nirupa Roy** are likely to be **cries** about her baby being separated at birth when some mob ransacked her locality. But one line that has it all, some *roar*, some *vengeance*, some *glee* and some *cries,* is: '*You'll regret the day you were born.*' At the REC Rourkela Boys Hostel, this wasn't just *reels*, it was *real* too! On my birthday, I would indeed regret the day I was born!

The hostel boys were paupers most of the time. But they made sure that lack of pennies and funds never came in the way of birthday celebrations. Come midnight and the *blessing brigade* comprising mainly of those who were itching the most to bless the birthday boy, would race towards his room where the birthday boy would ideally be oiling his back. For what was coming up was sheer boots!

When the clock struck 12, the birthday boy would first be escorted to the hostel corridor right next to his room to have ample space for the ceremony to begin. A few boys from the *blessing brigade* would hold him by his hands, some by his legs, yet others with his head. The boy who was born on this day some year would now be parallel to the floor, couple feet above. He would be facing up, and the corridor roof would come in the way of his clear view of the stars above. And then the honors would begin. 1, 2, 3… would go the count, ending no earlier than 18, 19, 20… signifying how many times the Earth had occupied that position it was occupying today with respect to the sun from the day the boy was born. And every count would be a thud on his *Centre of Gravity* (**CG**) in that position, hit as belligerently as though a hammer was being test-readied for crushing road rollers! For a moment, the roof would all disappear, getting the birthday boy to have an unobstructed and clear view of the stars above!

Not because of any stomach disorder nor fasting, but the boy would be on a **liquid** diet on his birthday because his tested-ok and **ghastly** swollen 'hammer' would need a cooling period before it could deal with **solids**!

The five minutes of midnight consecration (Hindi: *abhishek*) would be rife with 101 virtues if not more. It would have *enlightenment* from the Bhagavad Gita: *so you sow shall you reap*. No wonder, the ones to shower maximum blessings on all other 364 days of the year would be showered with the most on the 365th, on his birthday. Many of these givers brimmed with *revenge* and *retribution* showing in their eyes, in line with: 'This is my time to settle accounts,' vengeful **Chemistry** on display at its brazen best! The *sow* and *reap* doctrine made it a fitting instance of Newton's third law of motion too: *To every action, there is an equal and opposite reaction*. Each thump on the Centre of Gravity (CG) was a **reaction** that was waiting to show following the **action** that today's birthday boy was part of when he went about blessing the birthday boys on other days.

After the midnight sanctification on this birthday, Naveen was asleep until late in the morning. It happened to be a Sunday morning, and a girl entered the hostel. It came out later that Naveen was supposed to start his special day in her arms. But having run into the *blessing brigade* the previous night, Naveen needed more of 'balming' than 'arming' and as a result, could not make it to the arms of his darling! The girl's entry into and exit from the hostel might have taken no longer than it takes a bulb to glow after you turn the switch on. In all likelihood, she had come to the hostel to hand over to Naveen one tight slap for having not kept his word. But what followed in the hostel after she left was complete pandemonium. Poor Naveen, his stars seemed to have gone horrendously wrong on this D-day.

Tossed by his friends the previous night and **flossed** by his sweetheart during the morning, if the stars and astrology were to be believed, Naveen needed some serious *planetary alignments.* After all, if *friends* and *well-wishers* could be as ruthless on this day, what to expect from the *rivals* and *enemies* in the days to come? Coming to the hostel pandemonium, there was a near stampede-like situation that took hours to settle. Boys from all corners, blocks, wings and all floors in the hostel made it to the ground floor (where Naveen's room was) as though that tight slap a while ago had echoed in every room in the hostel! Had an alien entered the hostel, the situation would have been less chaotic! 'A girl in the Rourkela Boys Hostel' was bigger news than *Pitamah* romancing *Madonna*!

So would be the hostel birthdays in the Boys Hostel. Now, if that didn't get the birthday boy *to regret the day he was born*, what else would?

Birthdays in Ladies Hostel

The boys; celebrators, or crucifiers (?) would take on the rowdiest Mr. Hyde avatar while celebrating the birthdays of the fellow boys in the hostels. From the most ruthless butt-kicks that would take a few days if not months for the bum-bumps to soothe, to the loudest swears that indeed sent a chill down his spine, the horrendous showers of love would indeed make the birthday boy regret the day he was born!

The same crucifiers in the Boys Hostel would show their Dr. Jekyll incarnation when it came to wishing the girls happy birthday.

Dressed and rehearsed well and shaven after a while, the boys would reach the Ladies Hostel (LH) anytime between 5:00 pm and 7:30 pm, the LH visiting hours. And if you found a few boys around the LH with greeting cards in their hands, they most likely belonged to Year II or III. Year I was not the time when the boys could dare something as ambitious and adventurous because that could mean carnage at the hands of the senior boys. Yes, **Ragging** had some loud-and-clear-without-exception rules of the game; the most glaring being about 1st year boys maintaining appreciable distance from the girls. On the other hand, Year IV was when the boys would mature and begin accepting the harsher realities of life that *Naukri* and *Chokri* were not for them. And therefore, partly by josh and partly because of stupidity—and it was quite abstract to draw a line separating the two—the Year II and Year III boys were most active!

The effort and preparation time in the run-up to the D-day was remarkable, if not ridiculous. Or was it? From the choice of the greeting card, to what to scribble on it so that it 'pierced her heart', there would be a team of boys at play working on getting Pradip to 'go, get her' on this day! By the third year, it was quite evident as to who all in the Boys Hostel could write poems of love. Pradip would approach one of them to get a poem written for her that he would go on to scribble on the card. This poem in the card, Pradip hoped, would be the key differentiator from the card that Sachin would hand over to Sreshta. The *Chandans* and the *Surajs* had established themselves as the poetry writers in the boys' hostels who the *Sachins* and the *Pradips* would approach.

Sreshta would ignore Sachin and Pradip every other day. But on this day when they reached outside the Ladies Hostel to greet her, she would be courteous. She would be smiling at the silliest of their conversations. And this would get the boys to fist their hands in jubilation, all to themselves!

Minutes after Sreshta returned to the LH with the card she received from Sachin, the ladies would convene. One amongst them would read the poem aloud for others to hear. The ladies would go on to connect the dots, establishing what **gharana**[5] of poem it belonged to. 'The poem **Sunita** received the previous month and **Anita** the month before, bore considerable semblance to the one **Sreshta** has received this day,' it would turn out! And very soon, the ladies would know that Sachin's poem belonged to the *Chandan gharana*; Pradip's to the *Suraj*!

It would be interesting how Sachin and Pradip would hold themselves up the following day in class. Sreshta had appeared alluringly caring and courteous the previous evening at six o'clock. This warmth had got the two boys to dream showers and flowers all night. But at nine o'clock the following morning, she seemed totally indifferent! In less than 15 hours, the effect of the analgesic would seem over, and the boys would be back to their normal ways: stop shaving for weeks thereafter!

Internet today has got the better of not just the calculator, the small little address diaries and the

---

5 Gharana is a system of social organization in the Indian subcontinent, linking artists by lineage or apprenticeship and by adherence to a particular artistic style.

cassette-Walkman but also of the **Chandans** and the **Surajs**. And how can we forget the birthday greeting cards that have been hit so hard by the e-cards? The gadgets, the e-cards and the poems-galore on the internet have definitely infused more sophistication and beautification into the air we breathe today. But none can replace nor match the innocence that Pradip and Sachin exhibited while being at the LH that evening and which only **Anita**, **Sunita** and **Sreshta** could gauge. Deep down, they too were sorry that they had to show a fair degree of indifference and apathy at nine o'clock the following morning because otherwise, Pradip and Sachin would run around with hearts on their heads to declare a wayside triumph!

A little more smile on their part, as Anita, Sunita and Sreshta believed, could prove fatal for the young hearts in Pradip and Sachin. And that would be quite contrary to Pradip's and Sachin's beliefs that they certainly deserved some more empathy from the girls the following morning! The world moved on; so did the Boys Hostel. But for the next week or two, Pradip and Sachin would be more thunderous in crucifying the birthday boys in the Boys Hostel! Their Mr. Hyde avatar would come back roaring in!

Summary: If one seemed to be the chief consecrator at the birthday celebrations in the Boys Hostel, it was likely that he had been a Sachin or a Pradeep at the Ladies Hostel in the very recent past!

Aaj Kya Hei Khaane Mein?

The hostel mess was the most unpopular entity in the college. The reason why its unpopularity stood ahead of college canteen's or the college professors' was because you had options to evade the latter two to an extent; not the hostel mess! Result: you could not help eating and swearing by it every day. Outside food was an option but with the pockets always riddled with holes and with even the at-most-slightly-better-than-mess-food kilometers away, crying about the hostel food in the company of a few other hostel boys was practically the better option!

Find and Win would the gravy tease you for solid pieces in a chicken, mutton, or paneer dish. *Idlis* could cause serious fatalities if thrown at someone in the heat of the moment. *Law of Averages* being the universal rule, something had to make up for the **hard** *idlis*. The aloo-bereft **weak** *aloo parathas* did. The sugar in the *sweet* was the lone reason why the dinner menu boasted of a *sweet dish*. All in all, forget the boys mingling with the hostel food, even the food items could not. The *dal* quietly making its way out of the *rice*, hundred percent and in no time, said it all! The *omelet*, the *egg roll* and the *egg bhurji* brought some smiles and healings to the eggetarian souls. But since these items came under 'extra', their inflated mess bills at the end of the month reminded them that it was time to pay for the smiles they wore when the vegetarians were sulking!

You would get that five-partition plate as you entered the mess. And this would be the easiest part; the real challenge lay ahead. Some *sabjis* (vegetables), one *sweet something*, a spoonful of *pickle* and the *veg or non-veg special* for the day would fill the four partitions. These formed the 'defaults' in a plate. Any of these stimulating your taste buds and making you consider having more would be charged extra. Grabbing a plate with the defaults was easy. But if you were to survive in the mess for the rest of your time there, typically 15-20 minutes, you had to be a mix of instincts, reflexes, maneuvers, manipulations, soft-spoken at times, thunderous at others and way more. It would start with the chase for *roti*. The mess boys would emerge from the kitchen from time to time with 10s of rotis in trays. The kitchen was barricaded during mess hours lest a mob of hostel boys entered the kitchen to run away with half-baked rotis or worse still, the dough. The boys would put all their might to pull as many rotis off the tray as possible. If it was not your day, you could well end up standing there for long, awaiting your turn to loot rotis off the tray that you would find the others do better that day. After you were done grabbing your share, you would turn back to run your sight across the mess for a vacant chair. You would see none available and worse still, no signs that you would see one in the foreseeable minutes. And you would realize how short-lived your celebration over grabbing two and a half rotis had been. Yes, half of the third roti in your plate spoke volumes of the hostilities the rotis on the tray were subject to at the hands of the hungry mob!

By this time, it may well have been 10-12 minutes since you walked into the mess. And many a time, the better of the contents across the four partitions in your plate might well have been licked and swallowed over. You would now be left with the once-warm rotis to be had with the leftover contents in the plate, and the irony: you would still be wandering around in the mess looking for a chair, hoping that someone finished his dinner just when you were passing by him. A bad day at looting rotis together with an off day at grabbing a chair would get you to recall many more misses in life. The notable would be the bad semester result and the most terrible love-life that showed no signs of take-off despite the best of ignition efforts on your part. The 'why only me' question mark on your face would say it all. And when you could finally grab a chair, the deflated rotis would be your mirror, mimicking your plight!

The account of an army would be so palely incomplete without the mention of its soldiers. Ditto with mess boys aka *butrus*. *Butrus* is an Oriya term used for boys who should ideally have been school-going for their age but are working instead. These were the boys who would be serving in the mess. The word *butru* is more versatile than you can imagine for even the fresher boys in REC were called *butrus*. Coming to the mess *butrus*, they were phenomenal. They would identify each hosteller by their roll numbers and this was the number they would shout out for the mess manager to make note of when you asked for 'extras'. And therefore, if you saw someone in the mess moving around with a notebook in his hand to note down these shouted-out roll numbers, he was the mess manager. The mess manager reminded pretty much the **soccer** linesman but with a *notebook* instead of a *flag*!

A time long gone, the Rourkela memories, tempered with the spices roasted in the hostel kitchen, cross by at times. And every time this happens, a smile passes by the lips. As a *butru* in Year I, I would have my own tantrums at picking and eating vegetables of my likes and dislikes. And 'dislikes' horrendously outnumbered the 'likes'. Thanks to the four years in REC hostel where the choice was no longer between 'like and dislike' but between 'life and dislike', I got over all 'dislikes' in life when it came to the edibles! Today, get me anything to eat and I would chew it down to a nub in no time. This is thanks to the hostel stay in Rourkela where every damn *dislike* turned to *like*; don't ask me why and how. Thank you REC Rourkela Hostel Mess!

Kya Angrezi Bolta Hei Yaar

Three years in England for higher studies was all it took for Prof. Swain to completely get over his Indian accent. Upon his return back, he was a completely-transformed man. His makeover was not confined only to accents but also to his political views about the nation that he somehow sounded having grown very close to and concerned about. In declaring,

"Tthhonny will tthake the countthry tthoo hell,"
Prof. Swain was presenting himself as that 'dude' (at
least he thought so himself) who cared little about last
names no matter who. In line with: so what if he is
the British Prime Minister Tony Blair? His 'conscious'
effort to deep-fry 'T' to make it sound 'TThh' every
time he encountered one in any word, got him to hit
some, miss others. **Result**: Prof. Swain stocked two
flavors of T – the deep-fried **British Tthh** and the
shallow-fried **Indian T**!

Consciously or otherwise, Prof. Swain was driving
home the point that he was 'outgoing' unlike most
Indian professors not only in REC Rourkela but just
about anywhere. Talking about an incumbent British
PM in a tone as informal, Prof. Swain believed, would
help him shed the conventional taboo associated with
Indian professors who only talk books, studies and
grades. By talking little about *Telecommunication
& Information Systems* in the first few classes, Prof.
Swain was positioning himself as that ambassador
of the West where life was not only about slogging
but also about having fun; where life was not always
about 'calling the boss right no matter what' but also
about calling Tthhonny 'bloody' if he so believed. He
dressed in jeans and a tee where other professors in
the campus didn't quite like the idea of this attire even
for students! Here was a professor who was nearest to
introducing the **Romance Period** in college, inspired
by the 1992 movie **Jaan Tere Naam** number '*Mana ki
college mein padhna chahiye/Romance ka bhi ek lecture
hona chahiye.*'

The 90s was indeed the time when going abroad was hailed a touch out of the ordinary. The boys and the girls were in admiration of an Indian who just behaved and talked everything they latently aspired for. Select branded jeans and sports shoes were awe-inspiring, way beyond what the hostel boys and their middle-class parents could afford in those times. In Prof. Swain, the boys found answers to many questions they of late had started giving in on. There would be a chair in the classroom that the professor could sit on if he so desired, but here was our sporty Prof. who would sit anywhere but on this chair. It could be by the table with his legs hanging that would present the most vivid looks of his sports shoes; at other times by the desks, randomly. The students were soulfully approving every act of his as it defied the clichés associated with the professor-fraternity who the students in most cases found monotonously stereotyped and sinisterly boring!

What Prof. Swain could not get over though—and this was because it was deep-seated in his tongue— was his innate 'vernacular' English accent. For if he spent three years in England that got him to call Tony '*Tthhonny*', he also spent 35 years if not more in his hometown that would not let him round all those square corners that had remained frozen for a good 35 plus years in the nooks and corners of his tongue. 'Bloody' for instance, still sounded '*blloddy*'. Overall, coming from Prof. Swain's lips, 'Bloody Tony' would sound '*Blloddy Tthhonny*', giving us all a simulated flair of how the 'McDonalds Burger' would taste with

'Imli ka chatni'! 'British' that he now thought he was, at least very close to for sure, he wouldn't think twice before shooting the F word more often than not. Just that his square tongue corners made it sound 'fcOk'. Many more words and phrases for which many of us boys had received whacks from teachers and parents during our school days had made us believe that those words and phrases were not becoming of a sane civilization. But they came so effortlessly and seamlessly from Prof. Swain as though our parents were woefully conventional and conservative. 'Third grade *b********' was one such phrase that he used at least thrice in every class; just that the British sounding 'thhh' in the word was outdone by the local sounding '***aaard' that followed!

Prof. Swain could not go uninterrupted with his criticism of bLLOddyTthhonny, for he also had to take us through the **Telecommunication & Information Systems** syllabus that he was entrusted with. But he surely brought some change in the classroom air that had long gone stale. Albeit temporarily, Prof. Swain surely could bloom some flowers in the REC Rourkela desert that until his arrival in India was all dull, parched, and lifeless…

Tala Tera Chabi Meri

During our Rourkela days, bicycles were an indispensable mode of transport. Anyone visiting civilization—be it the markets, restaurants, movies—needed a bicycle to ride until sector II. He would park the bicycle at the **Max Mueller Bhavan** parking and then board a city bus or an auto-rickshaw to travel further. Well, not everyone in the hostel owned a bicycle and the culture of lending-and-borrowing was rampant and acceptable.

I remember that late evening when I returned to the bicycle I had parked at the **Max Mueller Bhavan** parking that afternoon. No issues; the parking lot was safe and had no instance whatsoever of any irregularity. I reached the hostel and handed over the bicycle key to my friend who I had borrowed from.

Two days later, this friend came to my hostel room, pretty troubled that the bicycle I had borrowed from him the other day and which he never rode thereafter, was not to be seen in the hostel parking lot. I remembered where I had parked the bicycle and could help him locate it. The bicycle keys didn't disappoint and at the minimal turn of the wrist after inserting the key in the keyhole, the lock stood open. But alas! My friend couldn't confirm the bicycle to be his because it was not his. And at this, I realized the blunder! My friend's bicycle I had parked at the **Max Mueller Bhavan** parking that afternoon the other day was not the one I rode back to the hostel. I was annoyed at myself and sorry for at least two souls: my friend who lent his bicycle to me only to borrow unnecessary headaches and the owner of that bicycle who would still be grieving the loss (or theft he would have assumed) of his bicycle. I had no option but to ride all the way to the **Max Mueller Bhavan** parking lot to try my luck at whether the cycle I was supposed to ride that day but which I happened not to, still laid parked there. It was pretty late in the night, close to midnight, and riding to the **Max Mueller Bhavan** Parking that was a good five km or so from my hostel, I had all strange thoughts in the world crossing my head. The traffic was near zero at that time. As a result, nothing came in the way of any strange thought crossing my head. "What if the bicycle is not to be found parked there?" I could recall that the bicycle I had borrowed from my friend and which I left parked at the **Max Mueller Bhavan** Parking was way newer than the one I was riding. The worst scenario could involve evaluating the price difference between the two and compensating my friend with whatever it came to. "Why could I not be a little more careful?" was the thought that was agitating me further. With heartfelt agony and anguish for the guy whose bicycle I was riding, I could also recognize a tinge of angst growing in me, blaming that guy for having found only that space in the world and none else to park his bicycle. Obviously, this bicycle must have been parked very near to the one I had borrowed from my friend and that was one if not the sole reason why this muddle took place.

So the 15-minute ride got me pondering over a sequence of uninterrupted and unadulterated thoughts and this included the **Tala Tera Chabi Meri** thought: If key A of bicycle A unlocked Bicycle B, could key B of bicycle B unlock Bicycle A? And if it could, did the owner of Bicycle B try it over Bicycle A? If he did, I was in for some serious trouble. And if he did not, the poor guy would have gone through the pangs and miseries of being at the receiving end of cycle theft! The **Max Mueller Bhavan** parking was a safe parking place. On reaching the parking lot, I found just one bicycle parked there. As I tried the key, it turned wholeheartedly, unlocking the bicycle A that was my friend's!

No matter how sure you are or how many times it has been done in the past a key undoing a lock always brings a feeling of relief. But when you are on heaps of doubts and yet the key clears it all, you are on cloud nine. And there I was! Yes, the key confirmed that it was that bicycle (my friend's) that I had parked there a couple of days ago, but which I did not unpark. It was time I unparked it and parked the one I had mistakenly unparked the other day!

Many years after that incident, I only hope that there was no other key in Rourkela, a key C of bicycle C that could open the lock of this bicycle (Bicycle B) after I parked it there and before its owner located it back! I also hope that the bicycle owner visited the **Max Mueller Bhavan** parking one more time in the near future, to discover that God had heard his prayers to give that 'cycle thief' the wisdom to park that bicycle back from where he had apparently 'stolen' it!

When Nepal Considered Bulldozing India

Mahesh Paudel was on his knees. Someone on his knees in an Engineering Hostel would most likely be at the receiving end of ragging at the hands of the seniors. But the fact that foreign students were exempted from this fun and Mahesh being from Nepal meant he was exempted; he was on to something else. The Engineering Drawing Sheet lay spread on his bed in his hostel room and with his knees on the floor, he was busy completing a drawing assignment. Just then, the wobbling ceiling fan struggling up until then could hold itself no more. It fell on the floor. It was summer and that meant Rourkela was red hot. But the incident ran shivers into Mahesh, who undoubtedly had the closest shave of his life!

Where even a two-minute power cut got the Boys Hostel on its feet, a ceiling fan falling right down in one room meant absolute pandemonium amongst the hostel boys. It was less due to concern or fear and more due to forged angst. In line with "**our lives are in danger too, for this can happen in any hostel room, any day.**" Thanks to this unusual incident, the usually quiet and keeping-to-himself Mahesh was now a known face in the hostels and the college. Mahesh could not have reaped as much publicity in his four years of Rourkela stay in any other way. With the girls too seemingly concerned and relieved that the ceiling fan did not fall on him, Mahesh seemed to like it!

In modern times, news and stories travel on the internet and mobile phones. It will not take long for rumors to be traced and nailed in a distance of five boys' hostels. But back then, news traveled through the mouth. And with everyone adding some spice to the story in ways he deemed fit, any story, in a day, would get distorted to the extent that except for the main character in the story, nothing remained real. This story was no exception and many versions of the story started doing the rounds. One version that caught maximum traction with the hostel boys was that Mahesh had suspended the noose by the ceiling fan after the dismal semester result. The story elaborated further: Mahesh was hanging in the air for a while with the noose tightening around his neck when the sky fell, bringing down with it the fan and everything tied to it! Never short on stories anyway, the REC Rourkela Boys Hostels had one more to discuss. And this story centered on haunted hostel rooms all over India and the world where suicide attempts were successful, unlike Mahesh's!

Interestingly, Mahesh wore a slight smile on his face every time. What is interesting about people with such smiles is that you cannot make out from their faces what emotion they are going through, for they are always smiling. Coupled with the news that he had taken a drastic step, many read in that smile the symptoms of depression! It eventually took a week if not more for all of the boys across all hostels to be convinced that Mahesh had not tried anything as terrible!

Meanwhile, Nishant Sharma had an update. He declared that the news had reached the Nepal Embassy. He further added that because India had breached the policy related to the safeguarding of foreign students, Nepal was considering attacking India. The hostel boys knew this was most likely a rumor, but just to make sure they were safe, some of them started reviewing the subcontinent map to see how far Rourkela was from Nepal!

Pattani Babu

Pattani Babu walked across all boys' hostels—five in number then—selling peanuts (*Pattani* is the Oriya term for peanuts). In line with a lion marking a passage with its hooves, this Pattani Babu would leave his mark by clearing off the dust along the hostel corridors he walked by. This had to do with the effort he had to put in to drag and pull his feet as he walked. Pattani's right leg was always grounded and he dragged and pulled it forward along the ground every time his left leg moved one step forward. A loud yell "Pattani Babu, 223" would come from a hostel corner and Pattani Babu would be on his way to room number 223. Somewhat like the Indian Postal Service, whose **speed** you can doubt but **delivery** definitely not, Pattani Babu would reach Room 223, his very thick glasses notwithstanding. And whereas the ever cash-struck hostellers would toe the credit-now-cash-later line, the Pattani Babu would register every unpaid penny across every hostel room across every hostel in his head, to perfection. A different matter altogether that he had no means of recovery!

To an onlooker, Pattani Babu seemed careless about the world around him. He would appear struggling while walking along the hostel corridors. During our Rourkela stay, it was once to be heard that he was 58. But if his gait, posture, mobility and style were to go by, he was easily 20 more, if not 30. News also did the rounds that his youngest was four years old, proving that the volcano within him that the volcanologists might have declared **extinct** based on his outward appearance was far from **dormancy**, let alone **extinction**!

From his photographic memory to the ocean of information about the Boys Hostel that Pattani Babu carried, he was so easily a perfect spy material. From the decade-old illicit hostel demeanors to the stories of the haunted, he knew more about the boys' hostels than anyone else, decades that his visits spanned.

He would not engage in any discussion with anyone on his own, but when given space to open up, he would. They make biopics of known personalities and dramatize upon the realities to spice things up. A biopic of Pattani Babu would have needed no spicing whatsoever and would still have sold hotter than the hottest of cakes!

News trickled in shortly after we left Rourkela that Pattani Babu passed away. Not sure what legacy Pattani Babu has left behind in REC Rourkela; maybe his then four-year-old is now the Pattani Babu II in the REC Hostels. For those who remember having not paid the Pattani Babu—once or more, intentionally or otherwise—the silver jubilee get-together of our batch may be a great opportunity to repay his debts. It could be locating Pattani Babu II, or maybe arranging meals for the needy one afternoon in the name of Pattani Babu during our short Rourkela stay. By remembering him together and doling out that tiny bit to his name, we would pay a small tribute to a man who slogged all day, in all hostels, across all seasons. It would be homage to a man who symbolized *patience* and *self-reliance.*

Pattani Babu, may your soul find abode in Paradise!

A Trip to Agra

End of Year II and it was time for a two-month-long summer vacation. This sounded 'wow' but for the mandatory 30-days vocational training. Most students found it more sensible to pick the first 30 days for training so that they could be more relaxed while spending the remaining 30 with family.

I opted for summer training at Maruti Suzuki in Delhi where my brother was employed. Viren would do his training at Bhakra Dam in Nangal, Punjab, a few hours from Delhi. So we decided to take the same train to Delhi from where Viren would take another to his destination.

The first step for a hassle-free train ride in India is to reserve a berth. Not to blame everything on a population greater than one billion, Indian Railways or Indian Government, it was almost impossible to get a reservation if everyone in the college decided to travel on the same day, especially going to a common destination like Delhi. Still, Viren and I wanted to give it a try.

This meant standing in a queue for hours without knowing the outcome. As expected, the reservation queue at Rourkela Railway station was long. Standing in a queue such as this where the outcome was not even guaranteed is one of the most thankless activities that you can imagine. The only positive was that there were two of us, and this meant we could take turns to stand in the queue. At some point, Viren said, "Let me measure my weight on the weighing machine."

The weighing machine is toy-like equipment placed on railway stations with red-blue-yellow bulbs taking turns to glow. The device would have a base extension on the ground on which one would stand. To acknowledge someone standing there, the weighing machine would spin a small wheel inside the glass case beside the glowing bulbs. The expectation would be that you dropped the coin in the machine inlet only after this small spinning wheel came to a complete rest. You would hear some strange sounds and in a while, a ticket would come off the outlet. You would then pick the ticket to see your weight printed on it. On the other side of the ticket, you would see some nice greetings. It could range from a message wishing you 'a safe trip' to something more bluff-ish like 'Today is going to be your day!'

Coming to Viren's experience, he came back saying that the machine sucked the coin in but never let the ticket out that would show his weight. I had heard stories about glitchy weighing machines and had some ideas about dealing with those. Asking the men in the queue in front of us and the others behind to safeguard our place until we returned, we went back to the coin-sucking weighing machine. We gave some random punches to the machine here and there. To our pleasant surprise, a coin came out of the outlet from which the ticket was supposed to come. One more punch and the machine now greeted us with a ticket showing Viren's weight. The remaining punches returned all the coins that other people may have put in over the days. The number of total coins may not mean much, but it was the pleasure of having experienced something new. Anyone can buy mangoes from the market but the ones stolen from the neighbor's garden always taste sweeter!

Back to the queue again, the line was still moving very slowly. In those days, Indian Railways had just introduced computerized reservation. Using the computerized system had its advantages. One of them was that it was supposed to improve the speed at which the train reservations were made. And that would help cut down the queue size. But it was not always the case. Most people were the same old employees trained to switch from manually opening a logbook to using a computer. At times they would take minutes to find an alphabet on the keyboard. As a result, there was a perception amongst the people in general that computerized reservation was more time-taking than manual! Additionally, computer reservation was rolling out in phases and not all trains and routes had reservations done on computers. This train that we were going to board for Delhi was one such. The queue at the reservation counter moved like a sloth getting the queuers like us to be restless. At this, someone made an interesting comment: "*Ye admi to computer se bhi slow kaam kar raha hai* (This person is working even slower than a computer)." However funny it may sound, it was true to an extent. Having said all of that, the outcome was what we always feared. More than an hour in the queue following which we reached the counter, we found that there were no berths available!

It was now time to travel without reservations. It was time to arrange for a bunch of newspapers. Yes, newspapers but not for reading. For contingency, if we were forced to sleep on the train floor. There was always a positive that there were many other colleagues on the same boat. Close friends Maninder and Uncle were also on the train. Uncle (his name was Deependra) was a teenager just like us, just that he had some gray hair. On the train, some elderly person overheard us talking. He was there for a great shock. He said, "*Jab ye uncle hai tau mai appke liye kya hua* (If this kid is uncle for you guys, then what would I be)?" We consoled the person and explained to him that the only reason we called him 'uncle' was because we loved him a lot.

Uncle was from Agra, the city of the Taj Mahal! As Agra lies en route to Delhi, Uncle insisted that we all took a break-journey at Agra. Indian Railway provisions for 'break journey' whereby one can 'discontinue' one's journey for a day or two and then 'continue' without paying extra. So we were all obliged to Uncle's request. In Agra, we would stay at Uncle's house. Uncle's mom and sister were very excited to see us all. Uncle's mom told us, "*Mera lalla bahut seedha hei* (my son is very innocent)." All three of us looked down, just trying to suppress our smiles. Even uncle had difficulties hiding his. Aunty (Uncle's mom) may have quickly realized that we disagreed with Uncle's image at his house. So she said, "*Lekin aap logon ke saath rahte seekh gaya hoga* (Maybe he has learned by living with you guys)." Guess she thought 'we boys' had spoiled Uncle. There was no need to blame us, but to be honest, every parent thinks their kid is the most innocent. Ours are no exception!

We visited Agra Fort, Taj Mahal, and more. It was one of the most memorable and fun trips of our lives.

She Is the One I Cannot Live Without

Story of Year II: started Calm; ended Windy

The queues at most of the 19 windows were beginning to get longer. And if the discussions in the Boys Hostel centered on *the what-next moves*, the Ladies Hostel wasn't discussing *Beti Padhao Beti Bachao* either. The marked change from their *bleak* DD (Doordarshan) expressions to the *blithe* MTV's in less than a year said it all! Meanwhile, every boy—well almost—was beginning to get bestowed with an *added identity*. And after his first name, the one identity that distinguished him more than any other was this *added identity*; not his surname, nor his Engineering branch. The '*Chemical wala Rahul*' for instance, wasn't defining Rahul as much as '*Sunita wala Rahul*' was. After all, it wasn't about the *Engineering branches* anymore as much it was about the *queues*!

To keep pace with the race, the boys were getting more *tactical* in their moves. At least they thought so. The boys wholeheartedly believed that *impressing girls* was a cumulative process and that the points scored from impressing her today would add to the net *cumulative score* up until yesterday. The boys wanted to believe that a day would come when this net cumulative score would breach past the cutoff on which day the *Sneha* would be Rahul's! No boy knew what that cutoff score was but everyone knew that only one boy would reach there first. And therefore, it was obvious that everyone seemed to be in a hurry to be the first to reach there.

Meanwhile, the course subjects were getting nastier. Long gone were the first and second semester days when the subjects were milder. For instance, **English** (yes, we had **English** in Semester I) seemed so refreshing; thanks to our English Ma'am who would sprinkle some unseen talcum in the class by her sheer presence! Contrast that with the **Control System I** in Semester III, and the boys—already under pressure to add to the *cumulative scores* that still showed clinging to the near-zero mark—could feel the heat. From the *fragrant* **English** talc in Semester I to the *stinking* **Control System I** filth in Semester III, the boys wondered where this slump would end, or if it ever would.

Stumbling into Semester IV, it had been a while not just since the ship had left Semester I shores but also since the shorelines had completely blurred. Many started realizing that the ship was in the middle of the Atlantic with its compass showing worrisome signs. Was the *Bermuda Triangle* around the corner? **Neha's** *apathy* then and **Sneha's** *indifference* now sent many Rahuls on course to concede that they would die a *Brahmachari!*

The boys continued standing and waiting in queues at the windows where the locks—nearly all 19—were catching rust. As though this was not enough, the keys to these window locks remained as elusive as ever. The boys, who were until recently finding it all too difficult to sit at the study table, now started finding it impossible. And this reminded all of the *gyan* the legacy of the senior batches had shared with hostel boys during the time we set foot into the REC temple: *For girls, higher the education, shorter the skirts;* and *for the hostel boys, higher the semester, shorter the stints at the study table.* It couldn't get truer: There were three very ordinary and consistently *dipping* semester results to show and with the fourth showing ominous signs of a complete rout, the *dipping* trend was *here to stay*. The **B-for-Ball** *Basics of Electrical Engineering* in Semester II was now making way for the **M-for-Malacophonous** *Magnetic Induction of Electric Currents (Part I)* in *Semester IV.* On top of it all, it was also an open secret about how our seniors (the Year III boys) were faring. Their dipping trend in the semester exams showed worrisome signs. To them, life in Rourkela resembled that of a convict's, counting days for his execution! News also reached all that many of these senior boys were faring as miserably not just because of the *Magnetic Effects of Electric Current (**Part II**) in Semester VI,* but for being '*besotted in love*' with the **Snehas' Ammas** (Snehas' seniors)! Damn, even the *ammas* in this college were bereft of hearts...

Year II had started with *clearing clouds across the sky*, but the end looked far from promising. Entry into Year III amazed some but startled most others at the sight of those virtual and fast-moving labyrinths of turns that the folks—not confined only to the boy's hostel—had to evaluate carefully before landing their foot on.

The writing was on the wall: **Year III was going to be a stripper of a year...**

Year III: Started Windy; Ended Stormy

Bhaag Rathi Bhaag

Category of Being Cool in College (REC Rourkela)

First-year: *New admission*-Self-discovery of being a nerd and socially bore

Second-year: *Internship*-Vocabulary building aimed at getting rich in expletives

Third-year: *Masters*-Realize that the switch from curricular to extra-curricular is complete

Final year: *Fellowship*-Do everything you can – time is running out fast... very fast

Rajesh, Rathi and Dhiren, the infamous three musketeers, thought they had taken decisive leads in making their way into the Ladies Hostel (LH). Making their way wasn't about razing the LH walls on Harley bikes. Instead, it was about the coveted position in the hearts of the selected residents there they thought they had gone on to occupy. When years of intense hard work started showing some positive indications—and the boys thought they had all reasons to believe that the indications were indeed positive—the boys were just about anxious to do more; that touch more. It was an itch that would not subside!

The huge college campus and the spring in the air made it a great place to walk around in the evenings. More than a kilometer west from the Boys Hostel, the road leading further west, stood forked. The fork tines would then lead separately for a while before merging. At the point of the merger, facing east, lay the entrance to the LH. While taking a walk after dinner that night, the three boys were feeling restless and their pounding hearts indicated to them that the time had come to do something heroic if not revolutionary. Sitting on a culvert at the fork along the roadside, their strategy building went on late into the night, close to midnight. Nothing concrete seemed to materialize and the boys were considering returning to their hostel just when an Easterly, in all likelihood originating from the temple, got the better of their consideration. What followed was inevitable: a decision to pay obeisance at the temple of love (the LH)!

While the two separated-at-fork roads merged in front of the Ladies Hostel, a third, perpendicular to both, ran west. All in all, if you stood facing the LH entrance, you would be facing east. To your right and left—South and North those would be—were the two separated-at-fork roads racing towards each other and eventually meeting. And the road behind, the one facing west, was that third road.

To accomplish great things, we must not only act but also dream; not only plan but also believe.

The boys' belief was simple: to see the ladies at midnight where the college rules strictly prohibited guests at the LH any later than seven-thirty in the evening. It would be a certification to themselves more than to anyone else in the world that they were indeed different and that they feared none! With almost all frontiers captured, they knocked on the half-asleep security guard at the LH Gate. The request to the security guard, however, to have the message sent across to the ladies that their respective princes had arrived (on horses!), got the security guard to react as though the men on horses were plunderers! Just as the boys were on with variants of the tricks of the trades to convince the security guard that the sky would not fall if he relented, a white Ambassador car appeared on the third road. The sight of the gate crashers from a distance was all that the car needed to turn its dippers on. Zooooooom it accelerated towards the LH as though Veerappan and his gang had presented to the cops a once-in-a-lifetime opportunity to get nabbed!

The entry of the car into the frame got Rajesh to take off and down south he ran at a blistering pace. Carl Lewis would have finished a distant second had he been running alongside! By now the Ambassador must have been no more than 100m away. The fact that it was midnight and there was zero traffic—this

road wore a deserted look even during daytime—
Rathi and Dhiren had at most 10 seconds to decide:
join Rajesh in the sprint and get Carl Lewis to end 4th
in the race, or wait there and be martyrs. 10, 9, 8...
and before they could decide, time had run out. Three
of the car doors opened and many custodians of the
campus got into action. Holding Dhiren's wrist firmly,
a seemingly shaken and palpably bursting-with-anger
voice inquired what the two boys were doing there at
that time.

The game was over for the musketeers with
nothing, absolutely nothing left to justify. The self-
proclaimed roaring lions would now be tamed and
forced to eat grass. Before this could happen though,
Dhiren, in a fit of nervousness, freed his held wrist
with the severest of jerks and thundered, *"Bhaag
Rathi...Bhaaaaaaaag,"* as he began to run with the
largest possible strides. But before he could convert
his good start into a victory lap, the shaken and
fuming-with-rage colonel, shot his part: "Stop Rathi."
Realizing that he was on a blunder spree—first the
unruly attempt to free himself; second, revealing the
name of the gang member (Rathi)—Dhiren had no
other option left in the world but to give up the idea
of fleeing. He pressed upon the brakes. Rathi who was
momentarily tempted to consider the *'Bhaag Rathi...
Bhaaaaaaaag'* call, realized the very same moment that
by naming him, Dhiren had already unwheeled the
vehicle that he (Rathi) would have driven to escape!

The treasure-hunt game started from that one
clue 'Rathi' and very soon, the campus-custodians got

from the boys their names, addresses, year, branch and their complete information that they could so very easily publish on any matrimonial site! "Who was that third guy?" was one among the volley of questions to Dhiren and Rathi. Rajesh's take-off from ground zero was apparently visible when the dipper turned on. More so, the road running down south— on which Rajesh had taken trajectory—ran straight for considerable length before taking turns. And by the time the car doors opened, Rajesh was still seen running with heart in his mouth, which was clearly visible, thanks to the series of halogen lamps on the street, none of which was dysfunctional that night!

The boys were asked to meet the College Dean the following morning. And not without Rajesh! The three custodians were college professors who were returning from the Police Station that night following some unease in the city over which a couple of college boys were indicted. The professors were already aggrieved, concerned and disturbed about the levels to which the modern-day college boys were stooping. On top of that, they found some more loafers in the form of these three boys bluffing around the LH gate late in the night. Had it not been for their timely arrival, the boys could well have breached the LH security that night to cause havoc inside!

Even though completely deflated, Rathi and Dhiren pulled themselves to reach the turn where Rajesh was waiting with heron-kinked neck and bated breath. The three then, on way to the hostel— this time boys'—reached the fork where the Easterly had triggered all action. Sitting on the same culvert where the Nobel-Prize-winning idea of visiting the LH at the weirdest possible time had first originated, the three deliberated the strategy to adopt for the morning meeting. One outcome of the deliberation was to look as terrible as possible when they met the Dean in the morning. This was aimed at driving home the point that they were otherwise good boys and not the loafers of the kind they proved they were. Their terrible looks, they calculated, would depict their remorsefulness better and could be instrumental in influencing the Dean to slap a relatively milder sentence.

To the boys, the morning dawned following the night that never was. Besides the look-terrible strategy, they came up with a few more:

i) to not try anything smart in the meeting with the Dean

ii) to not respond to the Dean any more than asked for

iii) to get an assurance from the Dean at whatever cost it might take, and it could be crying out loud if required, that the incident would not be reported home (to parents).

Interestingly, it was customary of the college to keep a dozen home-addressed envelopes from every student, right at the time of college admission in Year I. These envelopes were primarily aimed at posting the semester results and mark sheets to parents. Some spare envelopes would update the parents of anything additional and exceptional that their kids achieved, experienced, or expertized in. For instance, misadventures of this kind!

To meet the Dean at nine o'clock in the morning meant that the three were convicted but the sentence was not known yet. It was now for the Dean to take over from where the three professors left the previous night. His tone and expressions wore shades of sorrow, angst, pity, anguish, annoyance, panic and just about everything that would make it all the more difficult for the boys to see eye-to-eye with the Dean. Possibly, the Dean had also spent some time in strategy-making for this meeting, just as the boys did, to make the boys feel that what they were engaged in the previous night was a criminal act! At times in Bollywood movies, a fight sequence involving the hero and the villain is set up behind scenes where scores of *dhishum-dhishum* are all that the audience gets to hear. The next frame would show one of the two having taken more of the punches—the villain that would be most times—with blows and bruises all around his face and body. The audience would not see how the punches landed; just the result. In short, not the journey; just the destination! 10 min after the soft *dhishum-dhishum* inside the Dean's cabin, the three boys emerged. Needless to say who the villains were!

The boys, nonetheless, came right on their herculean effort—more of a latent wish—to dissuade the Dean from having the communication sent over to their parents. The Dean would know better they thought, but the 'looking terrible' strategy might just have worked, getting the Dean to (dis)believe that the symptoms showing on part of the boys were just signs of growing up; nothing more!

The story did remain a secret for a few days. But just when dust seemed to have settled on the episode, there came a notice on the main Notice Board of the college:

****

Mar XX, 199X

REC Rourkela, Orissa

Notice

The following Year III students were caught in front of the Ladies Hostel on the midnight of <<DD-MM-YYYY>>.

- Rajesh XXXXXXX
- SXXXXX Rathi
- Dhiren XXXXXX

They are hereby warned to not involve themselves in acts of this kind going into the future. Failure to comply will necessitate strict disciplinary action to the extent of expulsion.

This notice serves to convey that the college management has imposed a fine of Rs. 100 to each student, to be collected with the tuition fee for the upcoming month.

Copy to/

- Dean, students' affairs

- Principal

- HOD, Electrical Engineering

Registrar,

(Nap**eon Bon***rte)

****

The names in clear and large fonts and the surnames with absolutely no typos whatsoever left none in doubt as to who the heroes (or villains?) were. It didn't matter what went behind the making of the story; only the three boys knew. But congratulatory messages started pouring in, whereby the three boys were not too sure about whether to acknowledge or disown the pats. Seniors and juniors alike, every boy in the college and hostel had some or the other spice to add to the story in the manner he deemed appropriate. The hostel was rife with many variants of the story. But one that read real and which sold more copies than any other, sounded action-packed, calling for a disclaimer: 'The excerpts that you are about to hear have been done by experts. We urge you not to try to duplicate them.' The story talked about Rajesh and Dhiren having climbed over the LH wall to be on the other side. And that just when Rathi too was near about done, a patrol vehicle passed by, thus halting the most spirited charge of the joint NASA-ISRO sun expedition!

Maha and Purush

When we began our life in REC Rourkela, Dr. Prusty was the Head of the Electrical Engineering Department (HOD). Where a reigning majority of the Professors at REC had donned an aura of self-proclaimed invincibility, Dr. Prusty belonged to the slender minority. At times, upset students would approach him as a last resort to work things in their favor—postpone an exam for instance, for which they were ill-prepared. In all, in a campus replete with 'Netajis', here was a 'Gandhian' who would shower petals no matter what you hurled on him. His cool demeanor could fight fires and many a time concerns on part of students, for matters ranging from trivial to serious would fizzle out, once they saw Prof. Prusty.

Prof. Prusty was soft-spoken and that was worthy of praise. But at many other times, the students saw him as not happening enough. It could be about complaints that they lodged about other professors. At other times, it could be about the lab and library facilities that these students found inadequate. What was interesting (and disinteresting too) about Prof. Prusty was that he lent ears to all complaints. But when it came to 'action', he was often found wanting. In all, Prof. Prusty was pretty much like that (cricket) bowler who did not pose any threat to a batsman but whom the batsman could not score against! This would get the boys to lose patience at times; they would intermittently wish for a change of guard. In line with: Let someone else take over (as the HOD). "For good or worse, things will change," they would want to believe.

REC Rourkela had a rotation policy for the HOD. One HOD would make way for another professor every three years. So during our stay at REC, the Department Chair position changed hands and Prof (Dr.) A.K Mohanty took the reins from Dr. Prusty.

Dr. Mohanty was very knowledgeable. Honestly, we could make nothing out of what he taught but his involvement in the subject during his lectures made us to believe that he was knowledgeable. He would intermittently smile all to himself while describing a topic and this made us conclude his intimacy with the concepts. Not comprehending the concepts in the professors' class could never be the yardstick for us students to measure how knowledgeable or ignorant the professor was. This was because we were clueless in every class; damn every. And therefore, we resorted to other empirical formulas like the confidence one showed for instance and how non-stop one could teach, to determine (and declare) how erudite the professor was. On this account, Prof. Mohanty won hands down!

Prof. Mohanty taught us **Power Electronics**. Partly because of the vastness and partly because of Prof. Sahoo who taught this subject in our college up until the previous year, the subject was rated number one in notoriety and complexity. Prof. Sahoo, who we had heard of as the *Gabbar*[6] of the Electrical Department went on a sabbatical just before we got into Semester V where **Power Electronics** was taught. Luckily for us, we escaped the wrath of Prof. Sahoo who was known for asking "*Kitne aadmi the*?" (How many were they?). Not more than 20% of the students from the prior two batches had cleared this subject—thanks to the '*kitne aadmi*' question from Gabbar that the remaining 80%

---

6 Reference: Sholay

had no answers to. When Prof. Mohanty entered the scene, the students heaved a huge sigh of relief. In the Prof. Sahoo era, many from the senior batches had given up on the hope of clearing this paper not because they were failing, but because the grades they could manage in the exam were horrendous! It looked 'all over' for many until Prof. Mohanty entered the scene as a messiah!

When the boys were still celebrating the departure of Prof. Sahoo from the scene, Prof. Mohanty's long and arduous classes began to cast shadows on the celebrations. He would teach non-stop and once he got into his groove, which he frequently did, he would go on and on for hours. That he was knowledgeable besides of course being a very senior professor, not to mention that he was now the HOD, no other professor would dare to remind him when it would be his (the other professor's) turn to take the class next. These other professors had to resort to some other techniques to have Prof. Mohanty reminded that his (Prof. Mohanty's) class was over. There was no dearth of volunteers amongst us boys for the reminders. So in the next class, the students said "time" once Prof. Mohanty's stipulated class time was over. Dr. Mohanty found this reminder unacceptable. Possibly disgraceful! "Who are you to remind me of time? I am the HOD. I can teach as long as I want," he went on to say as he banged the duster which bounced close to the girls' desks. The 'possessive' electrical boys could feel the duster hitting their hearts!

As there was nothing much that the boys could do about the long classes, they decided to go about other ways. Some boys stopped attending Prof. Mohanty's classes and the fact that he did not bother about anything other than his lectures, proxies started raining in the class. One student would give a proxy for four to five of his friends. Many others would go to class but leave after attendance from the side door without being noticed. Of the remaining who attended, many would spend their time on activities of their choice. After the attendance, the boys would fly paper planes in the class. At times the planes would end up near the girls' desks, ditto what the boys latently intended! The girls would fly the planes back to the boys from where those originated. And the game of fly-fly would go uninterrupted where Prof. Mohanty would be immersed in the concepts of **Power Electronics**. When professors show indifference towards what all is going on in the class—and the fly-fly game was a glaring example—the liberties that the students take, reach unprecedented levels in very little time. Our Electrical Class of '97 saw just that. And just when Ramakant picked the plane that had landed near him so that he could apply trajectory to it for the next flight, Prof. Mohanty caught him off-guard! *Chori karna jurm nahi hai, chori karte pakde jana jurm hai* (it may not be a crime to steal, but to get caught while stealing definitely is).

Prof. Mohanty's temper shot through the classroom roof. "I have seen you disturbing the class every day. Meet me in my cabin after this class," came the reprimand from the professor who was trembling in anger. Ramakant showed up at Prof. Mohanty's cabin after the class. By that time Prof. Mohanty had already forgotten why he called Ramakant. Ramakant realized that there was no point in telling why he was asked to report. After all, what was the point of reporting his act of theft? Ramakant grabbed this golden opportunity with both hands to get away.

Prof. Mohanty's classes went on with the new equilibrium: He would lecture, completely engrossed in the concepts and the boys would have better things to do. How else do you survive the same professor lecturing over the time allocated for 3-4 classes? Another variant of the Ramakant episode happened in the class when the students, talking all to themselves, lost track of the fact that they were talking very loud. Prof. Mohanty would catch the attention of such abnormalities once in a while even though those were regular occurrences. And this time, just as he had the other day, he screamed aloud, bringing the roof down. He screamed, "Despite my warnings, you all have been disturbing the class this entire semester." It didn't stop there. He lifted the chair and threw it down like a weightlifter releases the load after having raised it, rendering the chair disabled! The brutal lift-and-throw exercise got the chair to lose one leg forever. Enraged, he started leaving the class. Everyone was happy and excited that the day's class was over. REC classrooms had a dais where Professors would stand while lecturing. While leaving in haste, he stumbled upon the dais and nearly fell. He could recover from the fall but the stumble somehow reminded Prof. Mohanty that he had not taken the attendance yet. By the time the attendance was over, Dr. Mohanty had forgotten all the drama that had taken place moments ago. He started teaching again from exactly where he left a while ago: explaining the concept of AC/DC converter as though nothing had happened.

The boys knew very well that the weather was turbulent and any flight around the next two hours— yes, the class went non-stop for two hours—was fraught with danger!

Then came the final exam where students from three batches assembled to write the **Power Electronics** exam. Students cleared the exam, availing of the once-in-life-time opportunity provided by the absence of Prof. Sahoo. The long and arduous classes from Prof. Mohanty may have been a pain in the neck for us students but the result was rewarding. It was worth it, to say the least!

The Gurukul Gurus

Gurukul was a residential schooling system in ancient India dating back to 5000 BC. The students were taught various subjects and about how to live a cultured and disciplined life. To start with, their parents would drop them at the teacher's abode where the pupil would reside until they completed their education.

As for REC Rourkela, our parents accompanied us to this temple of education to start with and with the college professors staying all around the campus not far from college, the REC environment bore fair semblance to the Gurukul system. As the boys in the hostel would very soon taste drinks and suttas (cigarettes), life in Rourkela hostel had its share of differences too! Four years in Rourkela was replete with events and memories many of which centered on our gurus (professors) and therefore, a drive down the Rourkela memory lanes without visiting them would be so incoherently incomplete.

Interestingly, many of our professors were known by nicknames and not by their real ones. While the home pet names come out of love and adulation, the nicknames that professors get in colleges are usually driven by sarcasm, wrath, fun and notoriety. Nicknames could range from very apt ones to not as much. But the former, many a time, sound so fitting that they outdo and overshadow the real! Our Mathematics professor's in Semester I was one such. We never knew his real name because his nickname, which our seniors had bestowed on him ages ago, fitted him as much as the protractor in the geometry box set fits in the groove set for it! He was Prof. **Benefit**!

His name consecration must have happened in very little time after he joined college because every sentence he uttered would be preceded, accompanied, or followed by the word 'benefit'. "For the benefit of my students…it's in your benefit…benefit of class… benefit of college…benefit of weak students…our benefit…"

Except for a few, the professors in our college were sparing in using their English vocabulary. Those who were not too bad with vocabulary more than made up by nailing grammar right on its head. And among those who knocked the grammar down, some would go on to amputate its limbs! "Both of you three come here", "Come to my room when I am empty", "Open the window, let the environment come in", "Maintain silence, the principal may pass away"; were the Shakespearean lines coming from these professors now and then. And interestingly, there never was doubt about what the speaker intended to say. **To hell with grammar and vocabulary**—the Rourkela professors endorsed this viewpoint, downright and with aplomb!

"Electrical Engineering was the toughest branch". To put this as a statement could draw stares from other branches, but this statement had reasonable acceptance if not unanimity amongst all in the batch. If any other branch tried coming close to being a contender, the electrical professors' miserly ways in evaluating exam papers would play their part to leave those contenders a distant second! So, coming to electrical professors, there were the Sahoos, the Pandas, the Dashs, the Prushthis, the Rauts, the Mohantys. Some weren't fiery but would more than make up for this politeness while granting us marks in

exams. Then there was Prof. (Madam) Patnaik whose entry into the class would extend a canopy of shade that would set the young hearts racing! We had Prof. Sahoo who was said to have been smitten in love in his younger days and that explained his funny ways. He would grant marks in micro which essentially meant one had to score more than millions of those to make it 1 when one needed 35 out of 100 in a paper to pass the exam! Prof. Sahoo lacerated the boys to reciprocate what had been resonating in his heart for ages after that aunt turned his proposal down years ago!

An account of the gurus at the REC Gurukul will be incomplete without the mention of Prof. Pandey. He was a face in the crowd and a topic for discussion more often than not. And for wrong reasons! The rate at which he ought to have been completing the course as against the rate at which he actually did was another highlight of his strange and scary ways! Once, a couple of weeks before the end semester exam, when someone in the class reminded him that we were light years away from completing the syllabus, he was caught by surprise as much as we were: "I thought your exams are in July," he said. That was March and we had our exams starting in April! Prof. Pandey would talk about his real-life experiences more than electrical engineering. His practical knowledge-and-experience-sharing spanned how not-to-do things way more than how-to. The substation he was in charge of in a village before his professor days had once caught fire and he and his team could somehow escape the wrath of the angry village mob whose crops were destroyed in fires! Apparently—and which Prof. Pandey never conceded but his body language suggested—he was party to the fault that caused the destruction! He also made no bones about the under-the-table transactions that got his dear one to change branch at the end of Semester I. There were limited seats up for grabs when it came to branch change based on Semester I results and his behind-the-scene maneuvers could get his chosen one to cross the fence when many more able and adept jumpers were left behind.

Prof. Pandey once told us about the lightning arrestor project that our college was contacted for, to save the Hanuman Vatika Hanumanji in the town from the eventuality of lightning. The Hanuman Vatika boasted of a 74 feet tall statue of Lord Hanuman. We understood that the project was assigned to Prof. Pandey and from all his narrations about his experience at Hanuman Vatika, we inferred that the challenge was not as much about setting the lightning rod as it was about concealing it enough. Otherwise, it would have exposed the undoing of the mighty Hanumanji. People would have then said that the same Hanumanji who had once burnt the city of Lanka down to ashes in no time, all on his own, could now not even protect himself from a phenomenon as trivial as lightning!

The *navratans in* the Electrical Engineering department added up to way more than nine. Prof. Jamuna Prasad would be in a hurry to dictate notes; Prof. Routray in a hurry to claim that the question paper he set last semester (exam) would have scared even the IITians. Prof. Mohanty would reprimand a student to meet him in his cabin after class for the nuisance that student had been part of, only to forget about it a while later when the student reached his cabin. With his eyes wearing the instincts of a hunter and his limbs racing to the site of frequent lab mishaps—faulty circuit connections for instance—the lab assistant in the High Voltage lab was called *Cheetah*. If you were responsible for the incorrect circuit connections that led to the blast, then it was impossible to escape the limbs of the Cheetah!

Many years into the end of the most exemplary Rourkela stay, we look forward to hearing about them. Many would have retired and would not be seen on the campus but we would for sure put our ears together to hear the Cheetah's gait as we walk by the High Voltage Lab. We would pass by our classroom where Prof. Pandey gave us accounts of the misadventures at the village substation. We would hope that the farmers who had to be at the receiving end of the substation fire are now wealthy and more than willing to forgive him for any blunder that he might mistakenly have been part of. We would sit by Prof. (Madam) Patnaik's cabin in that canopy of shade, feeling sprinkled with the most divine talc that she had sprayed the air with and which we are sure is suffused in the corridor air till date.

Reproduce

"You will now be thrown out of the college. Go and serve the nation." This was not the marching order coming from the Colonel of the Rajputana Regiment. These were instead the words of Prof. Jamuna Prasad when we made a courtesy call on him at his office a few days before we were done with our Rourkela innings. What Prof. Prasad implied was that we were done learning the tricks of the Engineering trade and that it was time to apply the learnings! Overall, you had to do extraordinarily well to correctly infer what Prof. Prasad implied. Especially when he was conversing in English!

Prof. Jamuna Prasad would walk to the class with a stapled booklet of notes prepared no fewer than a few decades ago. Once in the class, he would waste no time in unleashing his dictation that the house-full class would note. 'House-full' not because the notes were outstanding, but because it took a toll on the students to write as much later, voluminous that it would be. And with the photocopiers far off and photocopying reasonably expensive for hostel boys, not to mention the class attendance that had to be 80% at the least, the boys would rather have those written themselves as Prof. Prasad dictated.

Prof. Prasad had a defective voice box down his throat and the words shooting from his vocal cords seemed to be catching the ones shot prior. And in a queue of catch-me-if-you-can word sets, it was not always easy to make out what Prof. Prasad uttered. **Electrical Control Systems** was the subject he taught, or rather dictated notes for, but no one seemed to have ever told him that his **control** on his tone and dictation was worse to none! When pressed upon repeating what he dictated, a rather annoyed Prof. Prasad, with frustration writ loud on his expression, would warn the students that they had to be more attentive if they wanted him to complete the course on time. And that this would be possible only if he did not have to repeat as much often! No wonder, Prof. Prasad was synonymous with: "Write fast, I have to finish the course."

Prof. Prasad was linguistically challenged in that his English vocabulary was of an elementary level at the most. But if his body language was any indication, he was unaware of this shortcoming. He was also completely unaware of what the students thought about his teaching style. One's limitations that one is unaware of are usually the fallout of allergies one has to social circles. The less you mingle with the world around you, the looser you would be exposed to feedback. Result: Prof. Prasad! Prof. Prasad took pride in the quality of the notes he dictated, and this would show in the intensity of his oft-repeated forecast: "Boys and girls, 50% work is done. 'Reproduce' these notes in the exam and the remaining 50% would be done too." What he meant was that having noted all his dictations, the boys and girls were done with half the work. What was left to be done—and that was the remaining 50%—was to 'memorize the notes without any brains' and have those written in the exam. In short, what he strongly advocated was: '**Commit** to memory and **vomit** in the examination'. 'Reproduce' in Prof. Prasad's *Webster* was nothing more than 'writing' in the examination!

Prof. Prasad's indifference did not end at English vocabulary and his teaching style. Half the class would flunk in his exam paper every year and the irky indifference showing on his face gave no clue as to whether he enjoyed failing as many, or if he had no clue of what it meant to fail as many! Srikant was a better witness of Prof. Prasad's indifferences than perhaps anyone else. Back from Bhopal where he had been to attend his summer internship, Srikant rushed to Prof. Prasad to tell him that he met his daughter and son-in-law there; hoping that on hearing this, the professor would jump in jubilation and perhaps hug him. This is an outright corrupt Indian way of influencing emotionally, and such emotional tricks work with some professors. Not with Prof. Prasad who said, "*So what?*" If 'being emotional' was about expressing, the only time the professor looked emotional was when he uttered his hallmark line: **"Write fast, I have to finish the course."**

Prof. Prasad looked relatively more interactive during viva examinations. This would be when each student was required to appear in his cabin to meet him one-on-one. Prof. Prasad would be considerate in welcoming the students to his cabin and would be courteous to each boy and girl by adding the prefix Mr./Ms. to his/her name. As us boys were used to rustic name-calling in college; in our opinion, it was 'too flattering' of a professor to garnish as much honor. The thought 'I may not prove worthy of this honor once the viva voce commences,' added extra discomfort!

It was Rajesh's turn to be in Prof. Prasad's cabin. The professor started with a warm-up question. Rajesh was asked to identify a component in an *Electrical Control System* circuit diagram. The moment Rajesh saw the diagram, he was sure about his cluelessness! In such instances, any boy would resort to some random gestures aimed at signaling to the professor that the question was just missing him at that instance of time. Some head-scratching followed some sorry expressions and Rajesh said, "I cannot recall." Only the boys knew that the 'I cannot recall' answers actually meant, "I have no clue whatsoever." The professor would anyway make out eventually by the end of the viva voce that the boys were clueless about everything in his subject, but the '*I cannot recall*' answers coming from the boys delayed this conclusion by some while, if not until eternity! Up until that happened, Prof. Prasad gave the boys the benefit of doubt, insisting that they tried 'recalling' the answer that was just 'eluding' them.

Sooner than later, Rajesh realized that 'not recalling' the answer was not an option he had and therefore, in a voice feebler than those of the hungriest of rabbits, whispered, "Th..r..mo..m..terr." It was like sprinkling a water droplet or two on a pan mounted on a high flame to sense how hot its surface was. For if it wasn't that hot, the burst would at most sound a soft pop. But not to be. Rajesh's quivering voice turned out to be loud and clear enough for Prof. Prasad's quick ears. And far from a 'soft pop', the result was a 'fiery blast'. The circuit diagram was about a traffic control system having nothing to do with temperature or thermometer! So when the component Prof. Prasad had asked about was a 'switch', Rajesh identified it as a 'thermometer'! In asking Rajesh to "get out of his cabin" Prof. Prasad still called him "Mr. Rajesh," making sure that his see-off was no less courteous than his welcoming!

If Prof. Prasad was a much-talked-about symbol of indifference, he was also an epitome of impartiality that wasn't talked about as much. For if Mr. Rajesh's messy looks—and most hostel boys wore this look out of choice—were to be a reason for having been thrown out of Prof. Prasad's cabin, the swift and sizzling Ms. Sneha would have met a different fate without a doubt. Not to be. Shortly after the Rajesh fiasco, it was Ms. Sneha's turn to 'get out' of Prof. Prasad's cabin. This time it was a different circuit diagram where Ms. Sneha was asked to identify a 'thermometer'. As if two wrongs made a right—and this included the first wrong from Mr. Rajesh—Ms. Sneha decided to call the 'thermometer' a 'switch'...

All in all, 'Messy Rajesh' or 'Sizzling Sneha' did not matter to Prof. Prasad. To receive a ceremonious farewell from Prof. Prasad, you had to call a spade a spade; not a 'thermometer', nor a 'switch'!

Electrical Girls: Saat 'High Voltage' Saheliyan

The REC Rourkela Electrical batch of '97 was the *neighbor's envy and class' pride*. There were seven girls in the class and although this bore a pathetic girl:boy ratio, the fact that every other branch would end its count even before it started—**Chemical** and **Civil**: two each; **Computer Science**, **Metallurgy** and **Mechanical**: one each; **Mining**: zero—Electrical was easily ahead and by miles! Had it not been for Electronics' count (of five), Electrical would have been home to a good half of the girls in the batch. If someone is wondering 'what so big a deal', ask the Mining boys from the batch what this meant and you will never wonder nor pretend to wonder, ever again!

At the beginning of the session, the girls were circumspect of new boys around. This was because the 'cautions' from their parents, particularly moms, were fresh in their memories and still echoing loud in their ears. No wonder every girl in the class wore the most serious look for the first few days extending well into months; for a smile, they thought, could be construed as a signal to mingle. And such an 'irresponsible act' would be so violative of the 'parental cautions'! The main reason, however, why the girls could succeed in their plans of keeping to themselves was not 'caution' as they believed it was, but 'compulsion' on part of the boys who were going through torrid times. The 'compulsions' stemmed from the fact that the semester-long ragging season was underway and going by the system that had been in place in the college for long and applicable to first years, drawing courage to talk to girls was easily a Red-Card foul. One more reason why the Electrical Girls were not looking high voltage to the boys yet was that fresh from plus two, the boys were still very sweetly and innocently entangled in the first loves of their hometowns that they had not got over yet. Overall, the mix of emotions, compulsions, and 'love' did not leave much of a space for the boys to think very far!

Come Semester II and the boys started to open up. The seniors had let them free from the clutches of ragging in line with '*Ja, ji le apni zindagi*' and many boys started to realize that there was no point in being emotional fools and remaining besotted with their 'first' love. The Electrical girls were now smiling at times and the boys found themselves basking in that warmth that the class air had up until recently so terribly been devoid of! Boys are boys after all – they ask for smiles; nothing more! In the meantime, the boys found the girls smiling more often. This got them to be surer about whose smiles they were liking all the more. And very soon, they would also get sure who else liked the same smile. Rajneesh and Vinoth went on to become good friends for this like-mindedness!

And then there were the only-accelerator-and-no-brakes ladies in the class. They would score marks as though hell-bent on crashing the system. Nitika and Anjali started their REC Rourkela innings in Civil Engineering and having mercilessly lacerated the first-semester exam, qualified for branch change, eventually landing in Electrical. But the momentum they ended up befriending in their build-up to the first-semester exam apparently liked their company, never to separate. The two ladies kept butchering exam papers up until Semester VIII. Thankfully there weren't 50 or 25 semesters, for that would have tantamounted to a 'mass slaying' of exam papers culpable of examocide (for the lack of a better word)! If we talk about marks and the ladies of the Electrical batch of '97, we cannot keep Debjani away from the talk for long. With the grit of Sachin, the competitiveness of Federer and the focus of Dravid, Debjani spearheaded the ladies' challenge in giving the Senguptas and the Harjais a run for their money in academics. Save some distractions towards the fag end of the REC Rourkela innings, Debjani was so very easily the **Arjun** of the class who could see the bird's eye and none more. The batch will also remember her for showing the REC

Rourkela Electrical Class of '97 on the IIM Map. She received more than one IIM call.

Then there was Remmy. She never distinguished between the fairly expensive Indian Airlines and the reasonably inexpensive Indian Railways. Remmy would fly to Aizawl to her parents as frequently as the hostel Boys visited Maheshji (for Maggi at Backpost)! Some girls *thought* that some boys liked their smiles; Remmy *knew* that one someone liked hers! But for her distaste for Electrical Engineering—and this was the case with the reigning majority in the class—Remmy would perhaps have exhibited her extraordinary oratory skills to a far greater audience.

Some don't mind being **noticed** but are not too keen on being **noted**. Rashmi fitted this description perhaps more than anyone else in the class. Marks in exams or conduct in the class, Rashmi would come second to none in consistency. Of school and college times, especially when the timeline spans as many as four years or more, recalling someone gets us to recall her closest friend. Rashmi was an exception to this rule. She had many close friends, not just one or two.

From the 1ˢᵗ year compulsions when they posed light years away from the class ladies to playing pranks with them in 3ʳᵈ year, the boys in the class came a long way. On the occasion of Ranu's birthday, the boys, always itching to take the abnormal route, gifted her a *pauwa* (**pauwa** is referred to a bottle of drink measuring 180 ml). Filling the bottle with Coke, the boys had worked overtime to seal the bottle as though it came straight from the *daru-ki-dukaan*. Unconvincing that the boys sounded to Ranu when they conceded that it was coke and not *daru*, Mahasweta joined the party in tasting the *daru* (or was it coke) to convince Ranu that it was coke indeed!

Mahasweta (aka Mama) was easily the most splendid balance of smiles, caution, prank, scoring marks in the semester exams and just about more. From convincing Debjani that life was not to be taken that seriously to feeling for the boys—that *boys toh boys hain, shararat toh karenge*—Mama was an amazing presence in the Electrical Class of '97. She was aware of the many who were fond of her smiles but her conduct and response to this knowledge was a very gracious mix of thoughtfulness, aggression, harmony, obviousness and subtlety. Jitu, Ashish and Sanjeev are all in agreement. Manoj agrees all the more!

To all ladies of the Electrical Class of '97: **You were incredible**. Your presence made the class a better place to be in. Your presence in the Electrical class of '97 gives a lot more meaning to the memories associated with the place and the time. You accommodated the boys' mischiefs so very often as 'another instance of *nasamjhi*'. You maneuvered your expressions umpteen times to ensure that you were neither acknowledging nor demeaning the smiles that came your way. And for the countless more acts of nobility that you know you heralded and retained all through, we thank you...

Electrical Boys: Who Says Bridge Building Is Civil Engineering

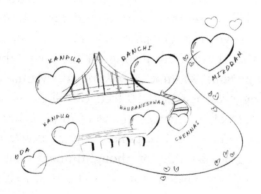

...Done with exams and I wouldn't worry about sleeping until late because my breakfast will wait...

...loving parents who would overlook most of my silly acts because 'I was still a kid'...

...a home I would not want to leave...

Such was life before Rourkela. Everything turned upside down in a few days as we made our way into the REC Hostel. And what all replaced were horrifying if not gory:

- the hostel *hungama* running pretty late into the night, thanks to the seniors' fascination for Hostel I where we 1st year boys resided. As part of the Ragging Mahotsav (festival), they loved playing with us!

- classes would start fairly early in the morning and that meant many managed to be in the class on time but at the cost of breakfast.

One week into the start of the session in Rourkela, the mamas' boys realized that the journey from 'boys' to 'men' had started. And if the initial signals of the journey were anything to go by, those were far from heartening.

There were boys and girls from *around the country*, hold on, there was **Vishal** from **Mauritius**, **Santosh** and **Mahesh** from **Nepal**; so that made it *around the globe*. They took a while to take leaps beyond their comfort zones to introduce and get introduced to strangers in the Electrical class of '97. And before that happened, the two Kanpur boys would live in a world of their own, always occupying the second last bench in the far-left corner of the classroom. Because each bench would sit three pairs of bums, there had to be one more in the world of Kanpurias. **Parishankar (Pari)** from **Andaman** that happened to be. **Pari** though looked as secluded from the Kanpurias and the rest of the class as Andaman shows in the India map! The **Tamil duo**—one from **Chennai** and the other from **Puducherry**—sitting right behind the Kanpurias had the Sikkim boy **Rahul** sitting alongside. Two boys from Andhra would come, see and leave the class together and so would the two boys from **Bihar**. The **Punjabi** boy from **Punjab** sat with the **Punjabi** boy **not from Punjab** and the Electrical class of '97 had no fewer than 20 boy-boy pairs! The girls came and left the class without disturbing the air as though they were non-existent. '**Men** are from all around **Mars** and **Women** from **Venus**' would label the Electrical Class of '97 across the first few weeks in Rourkela!

As though an instant geyser was at work, things caught heat very soon. Long classes, voluminous lab details to be submitted just about every day, terrible hostel food, seniors visiting Hostel I now and then (ragging) and more were the hallmarks of life in the new world. Amidst all this, the boys had to take to **bridge-building projects** too. A bridge-building project involved pioneering efforts on part of a boy to establish connectivity with a girl that could lead him to dwell in her heart! Chennai-Ranchi, Kanpur-Ranchi, UP-Bhubaneshwar were among the few such projects that stood out. But the one (bridge) that stood tallest connected the mountains of **Mizoram** to the Arabian Sea around **Goa**! On the whole, 24 hours started falling way too short for a day for most boys. By way more than 24 hours!

Some lived life to the fullest. Many believed this was mutually exclusive with the primary work they were in Rourkela for: **studies**. And there were still others who spent all four years complaining about the system. But the fact that everyone ticked and thrived or survived was because everyone found birds of the same feather! From Suvendu who would park his bicycle inside his hostel room for the fear that he may go cycle-less if he were not as careful, to Vinay who often saw *Shilpa (Shetty)* and *Raveena (Tandon)* in his dreams embroiled in *Dance of Envy* to wean over him, the Electrical Class of '97 had it all. Jitu and Manoj (Panda) were picked by the police on the New Year Eve party, not at the time of ruckus they were part of at the restaurant but when they visited the place a couple of hours later to assess what the after-effects of the ruckus were! Where Priyadarshee(PD) was the *Sergey Bubka* of Electrical Batch of '97 for bettering his own attendance record in the class over and over again in every semester and where Senthil did not bother much about his dismal class attendance. Then there was Himanshu who seemed to have come to Rourkela with a boon (*vardan*) to excel in two subjects that most others struggled in: **Engineering Mechanics (EM)** in Semester II and **Electro-Magnetic Induction (EMI)** in *Semester VI*! We had **Anjali** who scored a perfect 100 in the Semester IV maths exam and this score was what close to 30% of the batch took three semesters if not four taken together to score (in maths)!

If Ashish and Sanjeev had valid reasons to be at odds against each other all four years, Mahasweta and Debjani made the Fevicol pair, not just in the Electrical Class but in the entire batch! When together, while Debjani would often reflect 'concerns' in line with *what if the Earth stopped its motion around the sun*, Mahasweta would be there right beside her not to explain to her what would happen, but to signal to her that it was high time she stopped bothering about such worthless concerns! Ranu would smile back at you only when she could not evade your effort to greet her. Not because she intended to ignore or overlook but because she was of the view that the boys are boys and that they would at most have something useless if not filthy to talk! And there was Rashmi who sat right next to the wall on her right to ensure there was no disturbance or distraction from at least one side in the class. Eventually, news broke after the Engineering inning that Rashmi was a Sachin Tendulkar (cricket) fan! Is Ranjan listening?

There were some **e-BFs** (modern-day **B**enjamin **F**ranklins) in the class who had a fair idea of the concept of Electrical Machines on the whole, thanks to the diploma courses they had completed before joining the Engineering course. Unlike most others in the class, these people could actually see the electrons moving in a conductor when the circuit was turned on. Be it Abhimanyu or Suvendu or Aruna Biswal, their fascination for electrical machines showed gleaming in their eyes especially during the lab sessions. But how *ignorance is bliss* and how *knowledge can be one's nemesis* saw afloat in the class one day when Aruna Biswal goofed up big time. In the TDEP class (*Transmission and Distribution of Electric power*), to Prof. PC Panda's question about what the (electrical) resistance of earth was, Aruna Biswal shot through, "Infinity". Prof. Panda was perhaps searching for an answer of that kind because he was possibly not prepared enough for the class that day. He spent the rest of the class lecturing **Biswal Babu** (sounded more like **threatening**) about how answers of this kind coming from an REC Rourkela student could erode the name and fame of the institute which professors like him had toiled hard to establish! For everyone else not sure or who does not remember: Electrical Resistance of Earth is **zero**.

The story of the Electrical Class of '97 would go incomplete without the mention of Anupam, or would it? Anupam knew that his presence in the class was not a function of his attire. He would be dressed casually and not surprisingly, he let his grades do the talking. He came first in seven out of the total of eight semesters. Pankaj was another *yodha* of the Electrical class of '97. A supreme athlete, Pankaj kept physical speed and athleticism aside for the sake of Electrical Engineering. Besides those of electrical engineers and athletes, Pankaj possessed cells of civil engineers too. He too set sights on bridge-building!

Amit, Sankleet, Ranbir, Arijit, Jagannath and Virdi were some promising Engineers in the making in the class of '97 who knew why *Capacitors* blocked the passage of direct current in electric circuits. For most others, this was not as much interesting as playing Table Tennis in the hostel! Between the extremes—the promising Engineers in the making and those who had lost the plot altogether—were some more balanced souls. Deepak Nayak would perhaps lead this group when it came to a fair balance between 'Electrical Engineering' and everything else non-electrical. Venu was another. None in the class could boast of consistency as heraldic as Venu when it came to scoring marks in the end semester exams. He scored around the same total in every semester! Then there was Rajesh Ivaturi who was a good balance of *matargashti* and *sense*. Ashish (Saxena) was a good mix of studies, sports, humor, and confidence who utilized every minute to the best marginal return. Sanjeev (Khati) had the best pulse of how much time to spare on the study table – any less would fall short he knew; any more was not quite required! Then there was Swayam who wore charm. (*Swayam* rhymes with *Charm*).

And there was this *quiet* group. They would not add to the *shor* (noise) in the class because of their conscious (or unconscious) awareness that there were enough volunteers for this art. Interestingly, the *quiet* group had three subgroups. The first was front benchers (well, mostly). They were quiet to ensure they lent all ears to the professors' lectures. Rajula, Shyamalendu, Sudhakar, Sudhir, Chitto, Arijit, Jaggu, Rajnikanth, Srikant and Ramakant belonged to this subgroup. Sudhir *Serene* Mishra and Jaggu *Fundu* Tripathy – please accept the middle names. Then there was the second subgroup who came to the class for attendance and nothing more: Pradityu, Somay, Bijay, Manoj (Francis) and Karthik were the torchbearers of this subgroup. The third *quiet* subgroup made the best audience. These were the folks who would not shout out but would embrace and inspire the ones who shouted. Vishal, Rajdeep, Vipul, Dhananjay, Ritesh, Shalin and Rajneesh made this subgroup. Rajdeep was fond of football in his school days. But alas, he fractured his leg while playing football and thus came curtains on his football career. He, however, did not let this setback come in the way of his football dreams and despite all no-no from parents and family, made it to the football ground again. This time as a goalkeeper, for that he calculated would be relatively safer for his legs. But as though destiny had other plans (as they say), he saw himself off the football field again. A hard kick from a forward got the better of the stretched palms of the goalkeeper, fracturing his wrist! Shalin (from Gujarat) fared well in Economics. Ritesh spoke the Rourkela Hindi better than anyone else: "*Badi Bada hei be*," he would say to mean, "How big is that!"

In the meantime, by around Semester VI, many of these bridge-building projects that had taken off way back in Semesters I and II, started to show discouraging signs. These had never shown encouraging signs anyway, but of late these seemed going nowhere. There were signs of sabotage too. It remained no secret that many bridges were being built towards the same end. Interestingly, two or more engineers building bridges to the same end would each go on to make startling discoveries: i) my project is on course to being doomed ii) his project too! The two would then become good friends. Rajneesh and Vinoth were good friends though for different reasons! I don't remember who Pradipta made friends with! And then there was Ashish Paul who wasn't building bridges but had fair knowhow of how these projects were progressing!

Every good thing ends. The great journey of the spectacular 60 at Rourkela could be no exception. From the most incredible viva experiences to the fairly-oft realization amongst the boys a day before the end exam that they did not have the textbook, let alone the class notes, here was this special class of '97. From the fun all through the semester to a promise to the Almighty on the D-Day that 'I' would be a 'good boy' if He showered His love and blessings on me to score 35, just 35, the class was God-fearing too! From the disappointment at the end semester result to a feeling of slight comfort at realizing that 'my' friends had done no better, the Electrical Class of '97 was a wow! The boys leaving the stubble to grow wild in the hope that she would get moved looking at 'my look of dejection,' the class was also about strategy making. Waiting for the next Feb 14th because the one that passed by went begging, again, and that 'poem of love' on her next birthday that might just do the trick, the class was also about love and romance. On the whole, you had to be a boy in the Electrical class of 60 with just seven girls around to know the realities just about better.

Rourkela Electrical Batch of '97, we deserve a bow!

Hostel Ke Piche Wali Khidki

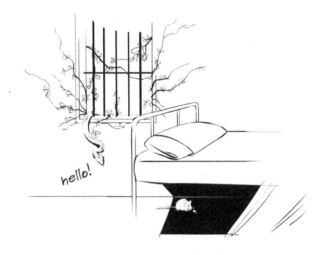

hello!

The Rourkela Boys Hostels—five in number when we were there—must have been beautiful sometime. Age, being low-on-maintenance and who-cares were the primary reasons why the hostels looked dull, if not dilapidated. Reasonably large, each hostel housed close to 300 residents. Spanning three floors with each floor organized into three wings A, B and C, the hostel had 9 sub-wings in all ranging from A1 to C3. Each hostel looked almost identical from the outside; just that Hostels I, III and IV had four-seater rooms, unlike II and V which had single-seaters. The hostels ran adjoining the *Hall Road* (yes, that's how this road was named, the *Hall Road*) that connected the Boys

Hostels with other localities in the campus. If you stood on this road with the hostels on your right, you would be facing east. The five hostels would make train bogies with Hostel V making the engine and I, the tail. A reasonably large lawn ran along the entire length of each hostel, separating it from the Hall Road. Lush green in select seasons but with tufts of un-mowed grass every here and there said it all: a hostel low on maintenance can never have a Mughal-garden-like-maintained lawn alongside!

The branch road, facing south, connecting the Hall Road to the hostel—a good 80 yards long and six yards wide leading to the hostel—had the hostel lawn to your right. To the left would be the boundary wall separating this hostel arena from the adjoining. The hostel wings in each hostel ran parallel to Hall Road with the C-wing on the farther side. The C-wing corridor facing the other side of the hostel had a four-foot-high brick wall separating it from what lay beyond. On the ground floor of this wing, a wired mesh stood atop this four-foot-high wall all the way to the roof to fence the hostel from the area further south that the hostel boys called the Jurassic Park. In all, the hostels had Hall Road on one side and Jurassic Park on the other. And Jurassic Park was home to snakes, *bichoo* (scorpion), *chachundar* (mole rat), mice, rats and everything you would not like to be beside.

The corridor wall and the wired fence notwithstanding, thanks to some openings on the floor meant for drainage, the *bichoos* and the *chachundars* found their way into the corridor and consequently to the adjoining rooms. Ramesh Reddy, who was otherwise used to the sight of these guests, jumped in shock and awe and brought the hostel roof down one day when he found a new guest in his room: a snake! It was no more than a couple feet long, but what went in the hostel over the next hour or so was disorder and chaos. Boys managed to pull the cot up that would now present an uninterrupted view of the serpent, but none would dare do more. It kept still with no trace of movement whatsoever, forcing everyone to believe that it was that ill-ignited Diwali cracker that might burst only when teased. Until then, the hostel—always searching for abnormal events to keep afloat and alive—found in the snake that perfect ground. The talks ranged from 'what snake species it was' to 'how not to deal with it'; 'how poisonous such stout, thin, narrow snakes are' to 'how to deal with snake bites'. In all, there were thousand expert comments; none useful!

Very soon, there were no fewer than 50 boys around. Boys from the neighboring hostels started trickling in too, but none showed up yet who would bell the cat! Or was it the snake? The fact that the snake remained as still as dead all this while gave enough indications that it had realized, albeit late, that its misadventures had got way too far that day!

Someone walked by with a pair of rubber boots. This marked the beginning of the end for the unwelcome guest. A reasonably thick wooden stick with a sturdy grip was the next to arrive on the scene and with the Plans B and C in place, the snake was tamed! It was now time for 'extra innings', the post-match analyses!

Amidst an avalanche of expert comments, the one that outdid every other was Ramesh Reddy's. "I am sure the snake had been there in my room for no fewer than two days." Ramesh's explanation stemmed from his microscopic observation. "Rats and *chachundars* spent hours together in my room until recently, but I have observed that over the last two days, they would run out no sooner than they arrived."

Ramesh had been subconsciously curious over the state of hurriedness of his old guests. And the snake story could finally allay his curiosity: The old guests would choose to leave Ramesh's room at the sight of the new guest, the snake.

Ramesh was right! A hiatus of three days and the rats and the *chachundars* who he had started missing, were back to spending hours in his room. All over again!

Yaar Chaar, Cycle Do, Kutte Hazaar

The REC Rourkela campus was obnoxiously huge and light-years from civilization. To go to the city, most of the time for movies and restaurants, wheels were required. With the campus not showing on the public transport map and with other transport means not to be, bicycles were the lone means of connecting with the outside Rourkela world. Only around 20% of the hostel boys owned bicycles though. This meant a group of five going for a movie would be four bicycles short. "I am going out", "Sujay has borrowed my bicycle...," would be the lines from the bicycle owners that the cycle borrowers would hear. All in all, arranging for as many bicycles could be a time taking affair at times and could eventually be the difference between the group going for the movie and giving up!

The hostel bicycles never retired; only changed hands. The passing-out boys would sell their cycles at throw-away prices to anyone who had thus far been managing with 'borrowing'. As a result, very few new bicycles were added to the aging fleet. It obviously would have been a thankless and useless activity but if an agency had studied the average age of the bicycles in the boys' hostels (there were five in all), the number may not have been far from the average age of the hostel boys. What stole the show in the two-wheeler hostel parking lot though were two mopeds (Luna) and one scooter. It didn't matter that the scrap yards would not find any of their parts re-saleable. What mattered was that those were motorbikes!

The motor-bike borrowing rules were simple. Because there was nothing left in these motorbikes to lose, the owners never had to apply any thoughts in lending out. All that a borrower had to do was to fill as much petrol as he would ride for. Not many boys knew how to ride motorbikes and the fact that petrol was too expensive an affair for the always-short-on-cash hostel boys, these bikes showed parked in the hostel parking lot most times as an elephant would in front of a *haveli*!

It was campus-placement time and **Arijit**, **Ashish**, **Sanjeev** and **Ranbir** made it through. In the hostel lingo, it was 'treat time': the job getters would throw a party. The occasion was no ordinary, calling for a celebration that by no means could be ordinary. It was time to spare some saved pennies on petrol. It was time to borrow bikes. It was time to ride to the restaurant in a way different from any bygone occasion. And why not?

With the second Luna just not responding to the most herculean kicking efforts, seven boys decided to manage with the remaining two bikes: one Luna and one scooter. Mind you, it was a special occasion and therefore, bicycles had no place at the party that night! There were seven in all to go to the 'treat'. The compromise formula which everyone thought was reasonable, was that four of them would get on to the scooter and the remaining three on the Luna. After all, a scooter could ride three anyway; so one more rider was not very big a deal. Similar story for Luna: a Luna could ride two anyway; so one more could not be such big a deal. And the seven took off. It didn't matter that the speed of the overloaded and on-ventilator scooter—that could fly 30 km per hour at the most with two riders—was at most 20 that evening! Luna's, 15! It didn't even matter that many other riders on bicycles were overtaking the two!

Rides for passengers behind the first pillion rider may look interesting, but it is not. You aren't camel high above the ground and with no place in the world to rest your feet upon, you end up carrying your feet lest the ground keeps those back! Between the scooter and the Luna, the scooter is a touch better. It has some margins whereby the first pillion rider can stretch his legs to rest on the flat area around the driver's, thereby making room for the second pillion rider to use the footrest meant for the first. But this bike ride had the fourth rider and all that he could do was to hope that the ride ended before his legs did! The Luna's story is all the more tragic for the pillion riders beyond the second. As it is, the Luna is very nearly grounded even without any rider. And with three, that very little gap whatsoever is between the seat and the ground, completely disappears. Well, almost! The third rider is compelled to bend his legs at knees beyond 90 degrees and with the two-wheeler gasping for speed all time and the biker applying accelerator to add some speed—that touch more—it looks perceptible to the third rider at the back that the Luna may trip on the rear wheel, anytime!

The seven finally reached the restaurant (**Madhuban**) in what looked out to be a mountaineering expedition and it was 'treat time'. But after getting down from the bikes, only five out of the seven could stand on their own. The other two needed to hold on to support. These two were the back-most riders on the bikes, one on the scooter and the other on the Luna and their legs had given in to complete numbness (*pins and needles*)! It took them a while to recover but in this time, they ensured that they reached a deal with the rest: while returning, they would not oblige the same seats on the bikes!

At **Madhuban**, the atmosphere was different than it usually had been with the same set of people in the past. The job getters appeared content in life and sounded generous: "Stuff yourselves!" It was a great party and everything went by script. It was now time to return to the hostel. And it was time to come right on the seating arrangements on the bikes. **Himanshu** had had it enough at the back of the scooter while riding to **Madhuban**, just as **Rajneesh** had on Luna. Result: **Arijit** would now be the *pin and needles* contender on the scooter; **Shalin**, on the Luna!

A six-km bicycle ride from the hostel to Madhuban usually took no more than 20-25 min; on this day though, the bikes had taken a touch more, rounding off to 30 min! And therefore, while returning, other than the seating arrangement it was time to come right on the route too. There was one route through the backyards that would bring some respite to the riders for two reasons: a) the route was marginally shorter b) the route was relatively free from traffic and that was welcome news for the far-from-proficient bike riders!

The riders started well and the learnings from the '**to Madhuban**' journey helped. This included the small adjustments each made to the share of his seat, besides some other tweaks and tunings on the footrests that could make life easier for others. **Himanshu**, now sandwiched between **Ashish** and **Arijit**, found breathing a touch difficult but this was better than being at the 'brink of offloaded' from the scooter every time a hump came in their way while riding to **Madhuban**. His Luna counterpart **Rajneesh** too had his share of good and bad on being upgraded from his rear-most position on Luna. Now seated in the middle, Rajneesh still believed that the Luna could trip over on the rear wheels. But the fact that he would now have a cushion in **Shalin** behind (or beneath?), made him all the more magnanimous in letting **Shalin** get some more seat space. Even if that meant pushing himself forward to the extent that **Sanjeev** who was driving the Luna, found himself not far from the front wheel! What could have been visibly funny but was not because it was dark and not quite visible, was that Shalin folded his pants right up till his knees to salvage his only party wear from dust and dirt on the road.

As it was dark and the fact that this route could not have had streetlights, the ride to the hostel was bound to be challenging. What was un-interestingly interesting was that the Luna headlights worked on the principle of the dynamo, meaning the brightness of the headlight was directly proportional to the vehicle's speed. There were half a dozen if not more reasons why the Luna could not catch speed, and this meant 'inadequate lights'.

The likelihood of something untoward hovered around until **Sanjeev** dashed the Luna over the legs of a street dog lying asleep by the roadside. The dog's cry woke up many of his mates all around and what followed was a **chase of fury**: a dozen dogs chasing the at-the-brink-of-giving-up Luna and the region was immersed in the **cries of death**: the **boys' screams** and the **dogs' barks** and it was a matter of time that the **boys' screams** were far outdone! The rather forbidden locality had in all likelihood made the dogs believe that it was their empire and in being stepped over, the dogs construed the dare as an intrusion into their sovereignty.

The three on-Luna riders had by now flung their legs high; parallel to the ground and the seat alike, wing-like, hoping that the Luna took the aerial route. Not to be! When in striking distance, the one dog—in all likelihood the boss of the pack—pounced on Shalin's legs. As though the dogs went by the rulebooks in meting out punishments and as though this offense on part of the **Luna-ites** had fallen under section 420 of the DPC (Dog Penal Code), Shalin was pecked with a kiss on his right leg. The fact that Shalin had kept his pants folded right up got the dog to get a nicer grip of his skin that would eventually take 14 injections to neutralize! What followed was one loud bark from the boss as though declaring to the world around that the job was done. At this, the group of dozen not only ended the **chase of fury** but also took an about-turn and walked away, quietly. By doing so, they asserted their supremacy in the region and let everyone know that any dare in their area would be dealt with, with an iron fist—nothing more and nothing less!

The Chosen One

If there was one roof under which diversity saw abound, it was the Electrical Class of '97. From the giant killers to the ones who preferred to let their actions speak for themselves; from scholars aplenty to poets swarming, the class had it all. One such talented presence was Abhijit's. He kept a low profile and would divulge more only in the company he confided in most and that was rather very small a group. Abhijit was exemplary in academics and this spanned his tenure preceding, accompanying and following all his Rourkela innings spanning eight semesters.

It was no surprise that his presence in the exam hall brought some hope if not a complete respite to his immediate neighbors. Such was his aura that even the faintest of his gestures and signals during the exam could help one cross the fence (score 35 that one needed to clear the exam). No wonder, when Abhijit had to once skip a mid-semester exam, our batchmate seated right behind him also decided to give the exam a miss. He had a valid question for himself: "Why take the exam and fail when not taking it up could not make it any worse?"

Abhijit always made people around him comfortable. He was respectful of the fact that the majority of students in Electrical Engineering were struggling and that even the toppers had horrid times. In contrast, you can't say the same about toppers from other majors. Take the example of Sid from Mechanical. After an exam, he was telling everyone that he fared badly at the exam and that he expected to fail. When the results came out Sid had 52 out of 80 which when combined with 18 out of 20 in the mid-term, came to a good 70 out of 100 which was a perfectly reasonable grade for the majority of students in the college. Abhijit confronted Sid, "*Abey tu bola tha fail kar jayega, fir ye kya hai?* (You said that you would fail, then what is this?)" Sid responded, "*70 out 100 tau fail he hua* (70 out of 100 is as bad as failed)." Sid may not have experienced the pain of electrical engineering students so he couldn't empathize but Abhijit had. So you won't hear a conversation like that from him.

Once we asked Abhijit how he ended up in REC Rourkela when for the knowledge and attitude he possessed, he could have made it bigger. Abhijit had ranked 42nd in the entire state of West Bengal in his 10th grade exam and 88th in his 12th. He was also a recipient of the NTSC (National Talent Search Examination) scholarship. It came out that Abhijit's dad had arranged for a professor from Presidency College, Calcutta, to coach him towards the IIT JEE. The Professor would give him give Physics problems to solve from *Halliday & Resnick* and *IE Irodov*. It was a no-brainer that Abhijit had difficulties solving these questions all on his own. Anyone would! After a while when Abhijit's dad went for feedback, this professor said it all. "*Engineering bhool jaiye. Dekhiye ki 12th pass karta hai ki nahi* (Forget Engineering, see if your son is passing 12th)." Abhijit was too talented for that type of appraisal. Despite that very 'dangerous' feedback which made Abhijit and his parents alarmingly cautious, Abhijit showed enough firepower to make it to the REC.

By the final year of our stay, Abhijit opened up and shared some more. He narrated an incident from 3rd year which for him was way more shocking and alarming than the feedback he had received from his professor in his 12th. What was interesting about this story was that it was way hotter!

Abhijit's local guardian was Prof. Das who taught us Digital Electronics in the 3rd year of Engineering. He was also a distant relative of Abhijit. After viva voce for the Control System lab where Prof. Das was co-professor, he invited Abhijit to his home for dinner. Abhijit had never known much about Prof. Das; had at most heard about him in family discussions at times. And from the little he had imagined and envisioned about him before meeting him in college, Abhijit was of the view that he was a *feku* (The term *feku* is Hindi slang for a person who keeps bluffing or does baseless boating). And this was all the added reason for Abhijit to be concerned if not worried when Prof. Das invited him!

As Abhijit arrived at Prof. Das', the professor seemed a rather cordial host getting Abhijit to feel comfortable. In the course of some informal discussions, Prof. Das mentioned to Abhijit that his score in the Control System lab was 85 out of 100 and that he had also asked other Electrical Professors to have a look at his marks. In those days, our professors particularly Electricals' were way too miserly in according marks which meant that 85 was outstanding. Abhijit never expected or wanted a favor but conveyed his thanks.

After some casual chats, Prof. Das showed some family pictures to Abhijit which included Prof. Das' niece who was doing Engineering in Australia. Prof. Das suggested that she would be a perfect match for Abhijit. Abhijit was shocked! He never thought he was ready for marriage. And understandably so. We were merely 20 or 21 in our third year. In a desperate bid to escape, Abhijit cited uncertainties around jobs that he had to think of first before taking on such responsibilities. To all such apparent misgivings, Prof. Das had the plans ready for Abhijit. He assured

Abhijit that the job was not going to be any problem. He said that in Australia, the girl's parents had very good contacts, and that they would arrange a lucrative job for him. The prof. added that even if Abhijit didn't intend to opt for a job, he had an option of working in his would-be father-in-law's company. According to Prof. Das, it was all dependent on what Abhijit wanted to do.

Abhijit was running out of excuses so he thought he should have this thrown back to his parents. He told Prof. Das that he was too young to make any such big decision all for himself and that his parents would be the right people to take any further action. Prof. Das played down this excuse too from Abhijit and referred to his own experience involving his marriage when he was supposedly very young. "Whereas you are now in 3rd year, I was only in my 2nd year when I saw this girl who was doing her medical," he said with a tinge of pride and pompousness. This was a double-strike punch from Prof. Das. He wanted to play down Abhijit's excuses as 'thoughtless' besides attempting to imply that he had been a lady killer in his college days! Prof. Das continued, "I just went to my parents and asked them to see 'this' girl who was doing her MBBS." Prof. Das added that he told his parents that he was going to marry her. His parents, as Prof. Das claimed, agreed to his proposal with no fuss! *"Jab Miyan Biwi Raazi,"* he said, *"...toh Kya Karega Qazi?"* (when boy and girl agree, none can stop them). By that point it had become *ek sawal, do jawab*. Every question or concern that Abhijit came up with was shot down with two bullets if not more, and Abhijit was floundering in space and gasping for breath! But Abhijit didn't want to go down without a fight and wanted to roll the dice one last time. After all, for Abhijit, life was at stake! Abhijit's cousin Satyajit was a few years older and had already graduated in electrical engineering from some other college. He had already secured a prestigious job in Rourkela Steel Plant (SAIL). Abhijit proposed to Prof. Das that Satyajit would be the ideal choice for his niece. According to Abhijit, Satyajit was a better choice hands down! Prof. Das said "Satyajit *nahi chalega. Tum hi chahiye* (Satyajit will not work; only you will)." Of course, **Abhijit was the chosen one**.

A sumptuous dinner would have in all likelihood been followed by some mouth-watering dessert including some Bengali sweet delicacies, but by then the atmosphere had become charged. Prof. Das let Arijit know that if he could get him 85 marks in his subject, it would not take long before the digits reversed! That the institute was autonomous, the professors had the final say in the marks and that would mean that the professor could not only turn 85 into 58 but could also influence other professors at doing ditto.

Abhijit had a world of thoughts running through his mind as he bicycled his way back to the hostel; completely unsure of what life had in store! He called his parents in Calcutta and the discussion reached his relatives elsewhere. One of Abhijit's uncles was too caring. When he came to know about all this, he expressed shock at Prof. Das' behavior and considered a Rourkela trip only to thrash him!

Meanwhile, it was an open secret that Abhijit had an affair in college. What was also known to all was that this affair was only 50% confirmed. '50% confirmed' were those affairs where it was all 100% on part of the boys, but with the girl giving a damn (which meant zero percent on her part), the average could only be 50%!

The story about Abhijit, Australia, the offer from Prof. Das and how Abhijit could reach Australia with absolutely no effort was too filmy and spicy to remain hidden from the hostel boys for long. To go abroad was considered quite big a thing in those days when the job market had just started opening up and the boys were now onto advising Abhijit that he was being stupid in remaining in love for the sake of 50% that showed no sign whatsoever of ever becoming 51! According to the boys, Abhijit should have been wasting no time in grabbing the Australia offer in what the boys thought was a 'golden offer'.

It had been a while since we had an update on this spicy but concerning ordeal; 'spicy' for all other boys but 'concerning' for Abhijit. We asked him how the story was faring. Interestingly, Prof. Das' wife, a doctor by profession, was practicing in a different city. That Prof. Das was still fairly young and that he had gone all out to marry her caring little what his parents or the society felt about it, it was obvious that he could ill-afford to live so far from her! He had applied for a transfer to a different REC which happened to be in the same city where his wife was employed. It turned out that immediately after that 'golden offer' to Abhijit, Prof. Das' plea for transfer got approved. And that meant Abhijit could get off the hook. Poor Satyajit whom Abhijit threw under the bus to save his ass, survived as well. It ended well for everyone.

Abhijit is happily married and doing well today. He has never been to Australia. Nor did his 50% success with his lady love in Rourkela ever get to 51! We are hopeful though that Prof. Das' Australia-wali niece could find a Biswa'jit' (the world conqueror) if not Abhi'jit' or Satya'jit'!

No One Knows I Proposed to Her

Story of Year III: started Windy; ended Stormy

Everyone in the Boys Hostel was now looking for that magic wand that would draw him out of the swamp. It was because they had long missed the *hard work* and *sincerity* bus when it came to studies. Seven **Electrical** girls continued to score as much in the semester exams as close to 53 boys could not. The story was no different in any other branch. The **Snehas** were eating *rotis* made from flour of a different *chakki* for sure! For the hostel boys, everything looked haywire. *Sirdi se Pareshan, Sir phatt raha hei, aur naak bhi bandh* – a yesteryear TV ad depicted their state better than any other. The ad showed how a **Vicks Action 500** pill would drive away all three nuances in one go.

And just when the boys were looking around for this magic pill, Aditya Chopra's blockbuster **Dilwale Dulhaniya Le Jayenge (DDLJ)** hit the silver screen. The film was a runaway in the Rourkela hostels among the Year III boys in particular. Mainly because the movie spoke in a language that every laggard in the Boys Hostel could recognize and a voice that everyone who had missed the hard-working and sincerity bus, could identify. Raj (Shah Rukh) doing woefully bad in studies, yet running away with Simran (Kajol) struck a chord with just about everyone. The movie was a multi-function wrench that seemed to come in handy for the girls too, not as much *inspired* by **Raj** (Shah Rukh) as *terrified* by **Baldev** (Amrish Puri) and **Kuljeet**. The writing was now on the wall: any further delay on part of the Snehas in keying the window lock for the Rahuls, could well be an invitation for **Kuljeet** to make it in through the backdoor!

DDLJ did to the boys overnight what months of dedicated strategy making could not. They could now imagine the Snehas on the other side of the windows, twitching and curling curtains for the first time. And to which the boys' claim and assertion sounded louder and clearer than ever before: *Ho gaya hei tujhko toh pyar sajna...* The love-bug-bitten boys conjured castles in the air, way beyond curtains, windows and *shehnais* but for that ruthless, cacophonic early morning torment, the alarm clock.

Damn! Every morning it would ring just when the boy found himself in the mustard field a moment away from weaving the *Tujhe Dekha Toh Ye Jana Sanam* magic. Shashank had taken a stride or two beyond this romantic number when the alarm rang. Dashed to the wall, that was the last time that alarm clock ever rang!

It was now the second half of Year III. The dipping graph in the academics and nothing-going-right-in-life notwithstanding—and there was no indication that any of these ever would—it was time to fire salvos. There had been a subconscious belief in the boys—and this was all based on parental and societal conditioning for years—that any shower of *love* to or from the opposite gender—would eat up all their time. And this could be disastrous for what they were most importantly in Rourkela for: **studies**. Not to say that no such belief would have by now got the Rahuls to be riding with the Snehas on winged horses, but it proved some deterrent in breaking loose. Not anymore, for there was nothing to lose now. Roaches and termites were reading *Transmission and Distribution of Electric power* in the bookshelves as the boys in the hostel rooms had a more important thing to do: rehearse for the D-Day. The D-Day would be when Rahul would say all, just all, to Sneha, "I have had to say this to you **right from day one**… but only for the fear of… I have got to tell you today how much I love you…"

The rehearsals would be *choreographed* by the few amongst the many in the Boys Hostel who were considered experts in Sneha-Rahul**ogy** and who Rahul confided in. These 'self-proclaimed and certified' experts were strugglers too but had a touch more experience in failing than the other novices. Just that these 'experts' kept all their failures to themselves, giving the world an impression that they were victors! Many rounds of *Live, Camera, Action* with feedback from the choreographer after each retake would mark the rehearsals. The feedback was aimed at making the D-Day line sound more extempore; less rehearsed. The preparations were on and the **Bastille**[7] was now a stone's throw from being taken by storm and razed.

The far west of the college campus, slightly mountainous and reasonably non-inhabited (boys called this area the **war zone),** was where the Rahuls would call the *Snehas* to hear them out. This would be to *tell them what they had to say* **right from day one.** And the fact that it wouldn't be restaurants nor any other public places had to do with the college culture and tradition: Expressing love and affection to humans of opposite gender in the open was against the basic tenets of civilization.

"I have never looked at you that way... let's be friends..."

As though he had slipped into an ice-well, Rahul would stand frozen, sedate and waiting to bleed white if cut at hearing this. He would have nothing more to say for there was nothing more that he came prepared with. The script and the rehearsals choreographed by the experts were so focused on *what he had to say*

---

7 Reference: French revolution

right from day one that it factored in nothing else beyond. And the moment she said, "I have never looked at you that way... let's be friends..." he would be caught off-guard. "Damn it," he would say to himself, "has the human population of six billion caught fire that I would pick you to make friends, just friends?" The excitement and euphoria of what could lie on the other side of the meeting had Sneha blushed and said "Yes" instead, made way for an awful thud. Alas! The astronaut had set himself up for the **star**; embraced the **meteor** instead, 'smitten' in love that he was! Or was it *first love?*

A deafening silence would engulf the war zone. Rahul would realize, aghast, that he had his face to hide from one, just one pair of eyes in the world at that moment in time, but the irony could not get any more mordant: those were the only eyes in the world at that moment in time he could not hide from. The *verses* had failed, and the *words* gasped for air.

As though a fall season had chanced upon the Boys Hostel, the campus was replete with heaps of tripped-over and doomed Rahuls: a toothless Rahul here, a spineless there; another deflated hanging by the air on the west side and one more sinking in the sink. The war-zone expedition was turning a *Jallianwala Bagh* for the Rahul-Regiment with every jawan returning from the battlefield wishing that the *human population of six billion indeed caught fire*. To these jawans, the 'let's be friends' line—that had at most sounded discordant to start with—had infused all deeper and was now feeling prickly in the veins: "She had better slapped me, for that would have resonated or echoed only once!"

Thus ended Year III. Quiet on the surface, the ocean was boiling within. And it didn't take quick ears to hear it all: Year IV was going to be about the firemen playing with fire with a message that said it all: *If you were allergic to smoke or phobic to flames, better stay indoors.*

Year IV: Started Stormy; Ended With a Resolve to Win

Kahani Puri Filmi Hei...

There is at least one similarity between *electrons* and *songs*. Each is a carrier; one of charges, the other of memories. *Pyar Kiya Toh Darna kya* gets even the most forgetful *dadaji* to recall his **Anarkali** which the *dadi* has always had reasonable doubts about. Mind you, the **Anarkali** is not the *dadi* most times! The song *O Meri Zohra Jabeen/Tujhe Maloom Nahi* still makes *dadi* blush when she recalls **this day that year** when she was spitting fire and which every member of the now-*dadaji*-then-husband fraternity around was desperate to burn in! On the whole, scale, rhythm, pitch and music take the songs to the ears at the most; the memories wrapped around them, to the hearts.

It was the fall of '93 when **Mohra's** music album was released. Those were the initial days of the REC Rourkela batch of '97. The hostel boys would go maniacal at the full-volume *Tu Cheez Badi Hei Mast*. The song's video would do the rest when the movie was released about a year later. The song *Alankar* (intro) *Dha Ni Sa* would set the melodic rhythm and the hostel would dance deaf-folded to the full-volume audio. Such would be the involvement that as long as the song played, the boys would become impervious to what might be going on around the world! If this song and its video set the hostel temperature soaring, the other one from the same movie, *Tip Tip Barsa Pani*, just about set everything on fire! The boys would shout the most emphatic expletives in reaction to the song to declare loud and clear that something, somewhere, was burning!

Then came **Baazigar** and the boys went into a frenzy for reasons more than one.

- The hero (Shah Rukh) was hooking two pretty girls (Shilpa and Kajol). At a time when the hostel boys could not draw the courage to even talk to a girl in the class, this Shah Rukh Khan act was unbelievable!

- The backdrop in which the song *Ye Kaali-Kaali Aankhen* was cast skyrocketed the boys' desire to take someone to party late in the night

- The murder that the hero made look like a suicide. A growing number of boys were turning *frustus*[8] in the batch and this terrible act struck chords with many.

- The title song *Mera Dil tha Akela Tune Khel Aisa Khela* that the boys rehearsed on bicycles in the absence of horses in or around the campus!

Playing this song on a *Walkman* clipped to their waist, the boys, riding the hostel bicycles, would position their hands in the air as though holding the bridle of the most gallant horse. It turned out that the bicycle got equally berserk, throwing Banaj off. Now you know how he lost his molar!

The **Baazigar** mania had not fully subsided when another Shah Rukh starrer hit the silver screen. **Darr**! The *Kkkkk...Kiran* struck a chord with the hostel boys. And the hostel sounded abound with **M***mmmmmm.....***Manish**, **A***aaaaaaaa....***Ashish**, **A***aaaaaaaa....***Amit**, as though it was completely taken over by the goats' and sheep's bleats (**mmmmm...aaaa....hhhhh**)! *Jadu Teri Nazar/Khushboo Tera Badan* played in the hostel in more than one variant. The song fitted the **Om Jai Jagdish Hare** rhythm and the boys often singing the song in chorus brought an air of godliness to the hostel!

Everything up until August 1994 had at most shaken the sky. But what fell on it in August 1994,

---

8 In the hostel lexicon, the frustrated-in-love boys were called frustus.

brought the sky down. **Hum Aapke Hain Kaun (HAHK)** turned out to be that hysteria that would get the boys to murmur day in and night out. And if you lent close ears to the murmur, you would hear them say, "No, you cannot stop me now." In **Prem** (Salman) each boy saw himself; in **Nisha** (Madhuri) each boy saw the girl he had been dating in dreams! If the **Darr** *Kkkkk...Kiran* (**mmmmm...aaaa.... hhhhh**) had turned the hostel a wasteland where the goats and sheep grazed, the **HAHK** *uhu-uhu* got it to be the cough-land where everyone coughed and with a smile! In *Pehla Pehla Pyar Hei,* every boy felt that the song had been written explicitly for him; in *Mai Ni Mai/Munder Pe Teri*, each boy saw *Nisha* dancing just for him. *Didi Tera Dewar Deewana* hummed in the ears and the hearts of the boys 24*7. The movie and the songs therein got the hostel boys to distance themselves further from studies for they felt the need to be more serious if they were to not die a *Brahmachari*! Every boy discovered that **Nisha** had started to stay with him a touch longer of late. In their dreams! If the Indian mood on **August 15, 1947,** were to be gauged, guessed, or simulated, none other could be a better representation of that mood than the one prevailing in the REC Rourkela boys' hostels!

The hostel was a cocktail of noisy fans, *fiki chai* and the most struggling bicycles. The hostel held **Go-Mi-Ch weeks** where the boys would dress in the weirdest possible combinations of the darkest possible shades of red shirts and yellow trousers; green trousers and red shirts, etc. to pay tribute to the pioneers of such combinations – **Go***vinda*, **Mi***thun*, and **Ch***unkey*! And it was only obvious that any movie touching around these variants of attire and language would be a runaway hit. **Rangeela** was. Besides the 'casualness' that the hostel boys were so easily friends with, the movie reinforced the belief amongst the by-now-desperate boys—that girls liked *taporis*!

The sky had been above the earth. Came **HAHK** and it fell on earth. It was now time for the earth to go up above the sky. And the release of **Dilwale Dulhaniya Le Jayenge (DDLJ)** in 1995 did just that. The movie got the boys to ride the bicycles faster, dress up better, shave more often, and more. Everyone was happy and this included those who did stinkingly bad in the semester exams, the results of which were out a week earlier.

For a month or so, the hostel became a paradise where it was believed that true love can only win. Interestingly, every boy also started to believe that because his love had been true, it was just about time that God would be kind to shower His blessings! So exuberant and lively the hostel had gone on to become that none talked ill of even Kuljeet! *In Na Jane Mere Dil Ko Kya Ho Gaya/Abhi Toh Yahin Tha Abhi Kho Gaya*, each boy found the second song that was written only for him. Some wondered how the Bollywood songs had started mimicking their lives. Boys were fond of **Simran** but **Chutki** too seemed ready on their radar! If **HAHK** had set the hostel mood similar to that of India's independence from the

British, **DDLJ** made everyone feel that India was now ruling over the British!

They say every good thing ends. How could the Rourkela stay be an exception to this rule? The highs, the lows, the fun, the sorrow, the loving, the cherishing, the forgettable at times and the sorry at others… everything marked the too-dramatic-to-be-real four years. An era it has been. It would be true to say that without those songs that came alongside the movies across those four years, the memories may not have been as garlanded or as vivid. The countdown to the most happening four years of life had begun and just as the numbers from **Mohra** and **Baazigar** had set the tone for the most exciting four years ahead, the end too had to have as memorable, as appropriate and as relevant numbers to chime.

None could have filled that space better than *Pardesi Pardesi Jana Nahi* (**Raja Hindustani**). The movie was released when the batch of '97 was in its final year, giving each boy another reason to believe that one more song was all about him; just him. The winks and the blinks accompanying *Mujhe Yaad Rakhna/Kahin Bhool Na Jana* said it all. The **Altaf Raja** number *Tum Toh Thehre Pardesi/Saath Kya Nibhaoge* was one more that would play loud in the hostels around this time. Boys would cry, and someone who had considered crying 'not boyish' up until then, would join next until scores of boys would be seen holding together, crying. For everyone knew in the subconscious that what was coming up after Rourkela could buy them *quieter fans, masala-chai, geared bicycles* and more, but not the repartees, the retorts, the wittiness, the nuances, the banter and the laughter that remained diffused only in the REC Rourkela hostel air.

Many years on, if something can still get us to feel that air and its fragrance, it is all because *Khushboo Kab Dur Pawan Se/Ye Bandhan Toh Pyar Ka Bandhan Hei/Janmo Ka Sangam Hai* (**Karan Arjun,** 1995).

The Musketeers

It all started in the summer of the year. We arrived in Rourkela in what we thought was going to be the start of a new 'honeymoon' of our lives: away from the restrictions of home, away from the sermons of the parents and elders who would always preach the path of righteousness. To dance and bask in the glory of the large and beautiful campus of REC Rourkela would have been the next thing to do. We started dancing and blithely at that for sure but to a different tune. Anyone else watching us would liken our dance to the monkeys' in a circus. The 2nd year boys had been waiting with bated breath for our arrival when they would wave their sticks to get the monkeys to dance!

They say adverse situations get you to determine your real friends. The ragging had been no better than wartime for us 1st year students but once it ended and normalcy descended, we realized how we had gone on to make some real friends. Here is an account of the most captivating and the most charming moments that we (Himanshu and Dhirendra) lived in our four years of Rourkela's stay and that would have been so disjointedly incomplete were we to not come across this close group of friends.

Ivaturi Rajesh

Rajesh had a flair for doing things differently. He was a coach on how to impress a girl. He would often say that if you wanted to impress a girl, then making an impression was very important; 'good' or 'bad' hardly mattered. "Do something so that she is thinking about you all the time," he used to say.

Rajesh had also devised a rating system similar to the ATP points that the tennis players are ranked on. An act from an interested boy that 'impressed' the girl would get him positive ATP points. For example, +100 ATP points. On the other hand, an act of stupidity that he would involve himself in and that fell flat would accrue negative points. The negative points also accompanied Rajesh's expert comments, "This poor fellow will never recover from the ground that he has lost today."

Rajesh had more stories around him that resulted from his belief that one must be on the move. We Electrical students in Year II interestingly had a Civil Engineering subject - **Surveying**. The **Surveying** practical was about a team of five. The class was divided into groups of five; surveying a piece of land using the instruments that we would get from the college lab. This included a measuring tape, chain, level staff and the heavy EDM, all packed in a bag. Rajesh's Survey group was truly international with people from Nepal and Mauritius. Even the people from India in this Survey group happened to be UBIs. UBI was the term used for 'Unfortunately Born Indians'. Those were the group of people who would only watch English movies, listen to English songs, etc. Rajesh was the only genuinely-Indian at heart. Interestingly (or 'weirdly', shall we say?), Rajesh's group ended up losing that hefty Surveying kit, even though there were five *chowkidars* (or students) who were supposed to be custodians!

Rajesh's associations with misadventures could not remain confined only to misplacing the Survey kit. He once borrowed a micro tip pencil from Gitanjali. His group mate Francis ended up breaking it. Because Rajesh was the one who borrowed, it was his responsibility to buy one and return it to Gitanjali. He proposed that his group (of five) contributed an equal amount to share the cost burden. Others in the group—who had neither borrowed nor contributed to the pencil breaking—disowned Rajesh's proposal downright. Francis rated such an act of doing so much for a girl as 'too sissy'. He responded, "*Abey ladki keliye* (All this for girl)?"

Rajesh was left with no option but to bear the entire cost of the microtip pencil all on himself. He had had enough and hoped that the story would end once he bought a replacement and handed it over to Gitanjali. Not meant to be. It turned out that the pencil that Francis ended up breaking was a birthday gift to Gitanjali from her father. Her father had associated the gift (the pencil) with being mightier than a 'sword' (pen is mightier than a sword, why not a pencil?). Gitanjali was reduced to tears when Rajesh attempted to give her the replacement. She lectured Rajesh, "You don't realize the importance of the pencil you broke." This sounded pretty much similar years later when we set out to watch the movie Devdas: "*Ek Chutki sindoor ki keemat tum kya jaano Rajesh Babu?*" She was very sad and told few other batchmates about Rajesh breaking the pencil he borrowed from her. I asked Rajesh about that. He said he bought a new one all by himself even though he didn't break it. His words were, "Why the heck did her dad give a micro tip pencil as a birthday present. He couldn't find anything better for the birthday? Tell me which dad gives a micro tip pencil to his BTech kid on birthdays?"

Rajneesh Gautam

Rajneesh had a flair for timing. His one-liners, often concise, summarized his views on the happenings around. These one-liners were often as fitting as the antique designs! He would say a single sentence, but that left a long-lasting impression that we remember to date. *"Ladki bahut kharab cheez hoti hai* (girls are a lot of trouble)," he would say in typical Kanpuria Hindi. "History has been witness to the most epic and devastating battles in the name of girls," he would add, citing the tragedies of **Mahabharata** and **Ramayana** and more.

Rajneesh's one-liners would bring us reprieve when the going would get tougher. Many a time, that one-liner would have been out of frustration and dejection. During the after-exam discussion, there would be more sorry faces in Electrical Engineering than those rejoicing. When everyone would be evaluating if he would clear the exam, Rajneesh would reveal another deep-seated frustration and this would be one polite rebuke to God: *"Bhagwan ko do-teen G* hi pyari lagti hai, jab mann karta hai maar lete hain."* I am not going to translate that but what he meant was that God was very unfair to a selected group of people; him being one among them.

One of our batchmates, whose style and behavior had a royal touch, made us call him 'Raja Babu'(king). Seeing Raja Babu in hurry, Rajneesh inquired what the matter was. "I am going to watch **Naajayaz** (Bollywood movie)," Raja Babu responded. **Naajayaz** means illegitimate child, so Rajneesh sarcastically asked, "Why are you going to watch your own story?"

Rajneesh had a knack for storytelling too. Just out from the viva voce for **Control Systems** from Prof. Jamuna Prasad's cabin, the frustration was writ large on Rajneesh's face. When pressed into describing all, he told us how Prof. Prasad had asked him to draw a circuit diagram about which he was clueless. Prof. Prasad, nonetheless, would not let Rajneesh go without drawing. So when pressed upon drawing "something, at least something," Rajneesh started drawing something. It was a circuit diagram, mind you, not the map of India. You had to have some idea to have the evaluator make some sense out of it. When Prof. Jamuna Prasad saw Rajneesh drawing this crap, Prof. Prasad went about screaming., "Mr. Rajneesh, what are you up to?" Rajneesh told us that he threw his pen instantaneously and told Prof. Jamuna, "*Main apne liye thodi bana raha tha? Tere liye bana raha tha. Ab tujhe he nahi chahiye tau fir jaa. Chilla kyon raha hei?* (I was not drawing the circuit for myself but only for you because you were insisting. Now, if you don't need it, I will stop drawing. Why the h*** should you scream?)"

Manoj Francis

Manoj Francis, the Keralite—tallest in our Electrical class of '97—many a time lived in a world and thought of his own. He felt men and boys offered more to the society and had his arguments to support this thought; if at all someone was interested in listening! He was an avid reader; spent more time reading books and subjects beyond Electrical Engineering. Few knew about his excellent writing skills and that was because he mingled with very few. He would also engage in experiments to discover 'the truth' about the effects of certain items on human behavior. For example, he would drink Coke with a Saridon (a pain killer). He was content with the apparent kick that this combination offered him!

One raw material that he seemed fond of was *Bhang*. Once, Francis consumed Bhang outside the REC Campus. He seemed manageable to start with during his return. But very soon, his hallucination got the better of him and he experienced flying in the air. He could have easily dashed in the air, but thankfully enough, he could subdue his illusion just enough and decided to walk, rolling his cycle alongside. When our classmates in the vicinity of our college campus inquired with him what that drama was all about— why the heck would one roll a bicycle when the tires looked all good—Francis found the situation the funniest he could imagine! Francis said he wanted to laugh but somehow thought it would look rude to the girl who asked the question. The following morning, students who heard his story agreed that it was the best decision Francis made in his life. Had he started laughing, he would not have stopped himself for the next few hours even if he wanted to!

Over time, Francis' experimentations got grander and reached higher levels. While he was in his final year, Francis conducted numerous experiments with *Bhang*. He once had a visitor from 1st year (we'll call him Munna). Being a caring senior, Francis offered him some. After all, *sharing is caring* Francis' experiments with *Bhang* had been about making the dose stronger. In other words, the same quantity that would otherwise have a subdued effect at the most would have kicking effects after Francis' innovative ways! What followed was worrisome, if not disastrous.

Francis found Munna's heart pounding as though it would come out of him. He (Francis) managed to arrange an auto-rickshaw that would take them to the hospital. Seeing Munna's state, the auto driver refused service for the fear that Munna might not last until they reached the hospital! Francis got aggressive with the auto guy telling him that he would instead drive two dead bodies to the hospital if he (the auto guy) did not relent! On the way to the hospital, Munna's condition started deteriorating – and this had more to do with the fear in Munna's mind than his physical condition. Munna had never consumed *Bhang* and all he had heard about the weed was that 'this was not for good people' Munna thought his end was near and he had one last wish to express to Francis: If I die, please do not let my parents know that I consumed *Bhang*!

On reaching the hospital, the doctor advised that Munna be admitted to the ICU. Francis realized that this was turning out to be an expensive affair! So he decided to tell the doctor what had led to Munna's breathlessness. "Looks like some notorious seniors forced him into consuming *Bhang*; the matter may not be as serious as it shows!" The doctor was furious at that imaginary senior. The doctor proclaimed he was very close to the REC Principal and that he would get that senior rusticated. Now knowing the complete picture and circumstances, when asked about Munna's health, the doctor said nothing was going to happen. Munna would be just fine once the effect and hallucination of *Bhang* were over in the next few hours. On hearing that, Francis silently disappeared from the scene. He had realized that any delay could be fraught with danger, to the extent that he could be rusticated! Nothing happened to Munna and he was discharged after a few hours without any medication. But Francis took the oath that going forward, he would never involve amateurs in his experiments!

The above group along with the authors, formed the Musketeers, the closely bonded soldiers. We (Himanshu and Dhiru) are very thankful and proud to have spent good and challenging times with the musketeers during the four years of our REC Rourkela stay.

Anunay Ke Bhayanak Sapney

We Electrical-ites were a class of 60. Although we attended the same class under the same roof and would be sitting at striking distances from one another, it took us months to recognize one another. The main reason for this air of stranger-hood in the class was ragging. Social distancing was rampant because this, the boys felt, could minimize if not eliminate the possibilities of thrashings at the hands of seniors. Overall, the more you interacted, the more you would be noticed. And the more you got noticed, the greater the likelihood of you getting lashed at the hands of the senior boys. So, the dominant strategy was to keep a low profile and remain as aloof as possible.

During the ragging period which spanned a good six months, we 1st year students did not have options on weekdays. But during the weekends, we had two:

- Stay put in the hostel and get whipped by the seniors. They would come in groups, at different times, all through the day and have fun

- Get away from the hostel and spend the time here and there in the market, towns, movie halls—wherever but the hostel—and stand a chance for some reprieve

Needless to say, we availed the second choice most weekends. There was a limit to which we could be watching movies because that was bound to be costly. But we had found a way out: we would buy the most economical (cattle class) seats that would be Rs.5 per ticket. We had some 'students' and 'group' discounts too that brought the price down further by 20%. In short, Rs.4 for three hours (one movie) to avert dozens of slaps was not that bad a deal!

This had been a regular affair during Saturday afternoons and all of Sundays and we thought the process had streamlined; reasonably good that it looked. Not for long though! Once we were a group of five watching this rather ordinary movie in a movie hall even more ordinary. Just then some boys from the back row could smell us seated in front of them. We

1st year students wore tamed body language during those times, no matter we were in the college, hostel, or the movie hall and it was no surprise that the senior boys recognized us. The movie hall was very thinly crowded—you don't expect housefuls for such movies—and this made their identifying job even easier. The torrent of teases that followed got us to wait for an opportune time to escape. That time came during the interval. It was there that our classmate **Anunay**, whom we had never interacted with before and who had come to watch the movie with a different group, recognized us and asked us why we were looking alarmed and escaping. We were in a hurry and just managed to tell him—as we were almost running after managing to get out of the movie hall—that rather than recovering the ticket price, the time had come for us to cut down on our losses!

Meanwhile, thanks to the language spoken in the boys' hostels, our internship at expletives was underway. When we arrived at the college, we had been exposed to only respectful words that we had used in the family and community that we lived in. But REC was a different world. Not a single line coming from the senior boys ended without a f* word embedded into it and sometimes multiple variants of f* bomb would be seen raining in the same sentence. We were also taught REC versions of songs, namaz, anthems, etc. which had nothing to do with neither our nation nor God. But for practical purposes, you can safely assume that those were R-rated contents. Initially, our hearts boiled in rage at hearing all and we wished we could take some drastic measures towards cutting the seniors to size. We wished we had the boons and blessings of the Hindu sages who could burn the devils to ashes; we would do that to the seniors we wished! But slowly, we started fitting in the grooves. We started realizing that hostel life would be so short of spices if we were to use the language we were used to in our families and communities! After a while, we got so used to those words that if someone didn't use them toward you then that meant he didn't love you enough.

In the upcoming days, we got to know more about **Anunay**. While we saw ourselves transforming and accepting the cuss words—at times even using those towards our batchmates—**Anunay** remained far from all. In those days, **Anunay** was seen wearing a finger ring with some strange stone/gem. In the beginning, we could not make out what he intended to do by pointing the ring towards the guy he would be talking to—he would often be seen pointing his ring towards the seniors—we made out soon that this was his way to deflect the expletives (*gaalis*) hurled at him. That meant if you called Anunay a **bas****, for instance, **Anunay** would, by pointing the ring towards you, deflect the *gaali* back to you. So you would know who the real **bas**** was!

Abnormalities cannot remain hidden from the hostel boys for long. And very soon the seniors too came to know about this funny magic! No wonder, very soon, **Anunay's** magic ring became the talk of the town. Senior boys thronged his room in huge numbers, asking him to explain how that ring worked. Seniors had also received the update that **Anunay** was pathologically allergic to *gaalis* (expletives), And this was enough for them to make him utter those words as many as they could make him do. Once during this attempt, a senior asked **Anunay** to fling five *gaalis* at the ceiling fan. "Kutta, Kamina,..." Anunay had not even reached halfway through when a senior interrupted him. "*Apne baap ko bularaha hei* (Are you calling your dad)?" he asked as he landed one tight slap on **Anunay's** face. **Anunay** learned the hard way that those words did not qualify to be *gaalis* in the REC lexicon!

Time flew at REC. It was a matter of time when **Anunay** too caught up with the language and tone prevalent in the REC air. Once, a fight broke out between different student groups. By the time college authorities reached there, everyone had already left. Unfortunately for **Anunay**, he was still walking around at the site. He was convicted as a trouble-maker for no fault of his and was fined. The justice system ran on the whims of judges and the college authorities had to convict someone; damn someone at the least. **Anunay** it happened to be! The college judiciary was also bereft of appeals. If you were convicted, there was nothing that you could do except to pay the penalty imposed on you! So **Anunay** took it upon himself and declared that he would now spare nothing he found around. Be it an opportunity to flick a book or two from the college library; at other times walk away with a pen lying on professor's cabin—**Anunay** would take anything he found in college offices, immaterial of whether he found those useful. His idea was to inflict as much loss to the college as the college had inflicted on him!

Our REC years passed by and so did **Anunay's** transformation. He had clearly come a long way. One day he affirmed that in his dream he had gone on to propose to a girl. What followed was horrendous! **Anunay** would go on to state how he was so thankful to the alarm clock that came to his rescue. For if that had not rung that morning thereby interrupting his nightmare, he would have found himself under a pile of sandals that came pouring from a crowd hearing him propose the girl! He had more nightmares to share in the coming days.

Electrical labs were known for casualties. Not the students (fortunately), but all our four years, we were witness to scores of lab equipment blowing apart. This had to do with faulty circuit connections that the students would be engaged in. The lab imposed penalties on the group responsible for such blasts to ensure deterrence. **Anunay** had a dream where he saw himself tied to a tree, with Prof. Routray whipping him with a long-roped whip, which a crowd witness to. As though this was not enough, he saw the crowd also pelting stones at him! There was an upcoming lab test to be conducted by Prof Routray. We sensed that it could bring danger to **Anunay** because, of late, his nightmares were turning real.

During the lab test, one had to carry out the experiment alone. Students were not supposed to get any help, like reference books, notes, etc. One had to memorize the steps and try to execute the steps in the sequence. Unlike regular lab where the entire group would get fined and/or reprimanded, during the lab test one had to bear the pain all alone. One piece of equipment used in the electrical lab was a Variable Resistor with a sliding rheostat. Most students were in a dilemma when it came to deciding where to place the rheostat to obtain maximum resistance, i.e., minimum current. Depending on single and dual wiring, one needed to place the rheostat at the start or endpoint of the Resistor accordingly. Not connecting correctly had catastrophic consequences.

In the lab test, someone connected the circuit wrong; he was warned to never repeat the same mistake. Among the second batch of students taking the lab test, someone repeated the same mistake and he dealt with a severe reprimand by Prof. Routray. Now was the **Anunay's** turn. He called upon Prof. Routray to check the equipment and the connections before he turned on the power supply. By that time, Prof. Routray had already lost all patience, so rather than checking or helping, he asked Anunay to perform a self-check instead. Left with no choice, Anunay, turned the power on. The rheostat setting was at a minimum, causing maximum current to flow. Result: the equipment caught fire. Prof. Routray kicked him out of the lab. His earlier nightmare of Prof. Routray whipping him came out to be true!

Anunay's tryst with extraordinary dreams and nightmares continued during our REC stay. No wonder, many years after he shared all, we still remember all!

Table Tennis on Monkey Ladder

One activity that uplifted the moods and spirits of the boys in the REC Rourkela Hostel the most, for participants and the bystanders alike, was Table Tennis. And there were reasons for it:

- Cable TV was yet to make its way into the hostel and that meant the TV viewership in the hostel was restricted to only one TV Channel: DD[9]. Those days TV had come out of the era of Krishi Darshan (farming show) but being the only channel that had to cater to programs spanning all spheres and all ages, it did not have much to placate the hostel boys running high on desires! Except for the few weekly programs and cricket matches at select times, most of the TV programs were boring.

- Such jingles as the Internet and mobile phones were hypothetical in that age; wishful at the most.

And therefore, Table Tennis had to be the oasis in the desert and the only subject the boys could find interesting. The girl-boy stories could have been another interesting subject in college but were not for at least two reasons: (i) the girls' number hovered around the dismal five percent mark in the batch and that meant a distressing scarcity of girls (ii) a whopping 80% of them had given their words to their parents that the Dr. *Fixit Waterproof Sanskar* layer that their parents had applied on them with that Enamel coating would not peel off come what may. With this **Sanskar** layer, they would keep miles away from boys. Unable to dent the enamel coat, the boys had not much to do beyond playing Ping Pong in the hostel!

---

9 DD or Door Darshan is an autonomous public service broadcaster founded by the Government of India, owned by the Broadcasting Ministry of India.

Overall, a look back into what all the hostel boys could have avoided to fare better in academics, **Table Tennis** would stand out! The time and effort spent **at** and **around** the TT table—**at** playing and **around** awaiting one's turn—was more than any other single activity could account for. For many boys, this was way beyond the time spent on the study table! In fact, a biopic of any hostel boy chosen at random is most likely to be ludicrously incomplete without his Table Tennis adventurism in the Rourkela hostel. If **hot drinks** made the most tenacious glue in holding the boys together, the hostel Table Tennis was a not very distant third; *sutta* (cigarette) being the second in the list!

What is usually interesting about Table Tennis stories in hostels—and this is far from interesting for the boys residing in the hostel—is that the tables are usually on wheelchairs! A TT table set comprises two tables that conjoin at the net. Each table must have four legs to stand on its own. This means the complete set comprises eight legs. You cannot expect the usually-unruly hostel boys, that too in a large hostel of over 300 boys, to be mild enough to the extent that all eight legs of the table set will stay intact for long. That meant we had to account for unconventional supports around the table to keep it from falling. The net would be another symbol of neglect and resignation and the poles and support around to hold it from falling would remind one of a patient in the ICU with the saline stands around! No wonder, setting up the TT table and the net was by no way smaller a task than getting a steam locomotive to run!

If setting up the table and the net was a task as **herculean** as setting up fire in the stone age, keeping the flame intact was by no means trivial. Resting on strange kinds of supports, the TT table was capable of withstanding only the weight of the TT ball on it. Any other gentlest of accidental touches would get the soul of the 'house of cards' to enter the TT Table and it would fall flat. Well, almost. And unless you were lucky, the net too would join the party.

Many boys who were indifferent to the table and net setup efforts would show up and mark their attendance once the setup was ready. And as more and more people joined, you would have to wait longer in that proportion for your next game. As though this was not all, the TT ball flying off the bat many a time would sit onto the strange beam extensions adjoining the roof. The hostel caretaker who issued the TT bats and ball would issue one ball and no more. One boy, any in the hostel, would have to get the set issued in his name and it would be his responsibility to return the set in the same condition. Summing up, one ball was all that the hostel caretaker had and that too would fly and sit on the beams! And that meant it was time for some serious acrobatics by the hostel boys to bring the ball down.

Boys would form a human pyramid (in the hostel, we called it the **Monkey Ladder**). A circle on the ground would be formed with the relatively heftier and stronger boys, around four in number. Each boy would lock his arms with the adjoining two, thus forming the first tier of the pyramid. **Three** strong boys not as hefty as those in the first tier would then climb the arm-in-arm footrest laid down by these first-tier boys, to form the second-tier. The lightest of the boys around—the **Spiderman**—would then climb the two tiers and stretching his hand while keeping his foot rested on the second-tier footrest, fetched the ball from the beam extension. The boy would be oblivious to the fact that he was a sneeze away from grounding: not just his own but of any seven below him! And hold on. It would be against the most ordinary common sense of the boy on the top to throw the ball down. Because then, one or more of the excited tier-1 boys could pounce on it in the hope that getting hold of the ball may well be the tie-breaker in deciding who will play the next game. Imagine the fatality this could cause to the **Spiderman**! Everything evolves and so did the Monkey Ladder. The **Spiderman** would hold onto the ball until the pyramid was completely grounded!

The resource brings convenience; absence of it, stories!

I Do Not like Girls

Story of Year IV: Started Stormy; ended with a Resolve to Win

Cometh Year IV, cometh the time to remember God. When 'mess' was not the word to describe how the boys were faring and when only God could help! Year IV had to be different from the three bygones when the little plane of life seemed helplessly and haplessly swaying in turbulence, constantly buffeted by tearaway wind. The same boys who had experienced some runaway academic success up until three years ago before reaching Rourkela were now aiming for 35% in each subject and no more. For they knew that for the effort they were able to put in, they did not deserve any better. "*But if an effort was the lone reason for success or failure,*" they would cry, "*God tell me, why the damn have I failed elsewhere?*" signaling to God that for the love and affection they showered on the Snehas, they deserved better!

Drinks in the boys' hostels were now getting a touch more frequent and God was so very often at the receiving end of the torrent of questions coming from the boys: "*Tell me, Lord, you know everything. What fell short in my prayers and conviction and dedication and reverence that but for my ability to speak like a human, I get a feeling that I have become a street dog? (Kutta bunn gaya hoon mein; haan, haan, kutta).*" Blame it on the Snehas' indifference or the Rahuls' fates, the Rahuls were now on the brink of barking. A steep fall indeed!

Meanwhile, the parents back home were still used to knowing that variant of Rahul who dusted exam papers up until three years ago. And to them, it was not a matter of *if*, rather *when* that the phone would ring or rather sing laurels about their hard-working *beta* making it through to the *Amrika wali company!* Year IV was campus placement time and the parents back home had been waiting for the 'good news'! Little did they realize that expecting academic brilliance from a love-struck boy was like asking a train driver to drive the train at breakneck speed when its coaches had completely derailed! Little did they apprehend that the Boys Hostel and college air was brimming with war cries emanating from the *war zone* martyrs and to excel in such air of melancholic musings was a far cry! Little did they appreciate that these *Advanced Engineering* concepts—way beyond the technicalities of the Engineering course—weren't a kid's play! Overall, little did they recognize that the Rahul in Rourkela had reduced to a lump of mud, and closer scrutiny did not rule out the possibility of the 'lump' being 'shit'!

With no derailments, no war cries, no undercurrents and no trace of *Advanced Engineering Concepts* to deal with, Engineering to **Snehas** was a click copy of the dreams the parents see of their kids who make it to a reputed institute. These parents had painted pictures of a highway that would take their *bitiyas* (daughters) to the *Thakur wali haveli* where the *Kunwar sahib* (prince) was waiting with garlands. And the Snehas seemed well on course on the middle lane of the highway having a good couple of lanes on either side as margins. This was in stark contrast to the boys who were just about clinging on to the road shoulder of the village road, a pothole away from landing into the deepest of roadside pits!

Meanwhile, the Kishore Kumar numbers were on the wane in the Boys Hostel making way for the most charred and heartburn numbers. **Sonu Nigam's** *Accha sila diya tune mere pyar ka/Yaar ne hi loot liya ghar yaar ka* topped the list, playing in some or the other hostel corner most times; just always. The hostel stay was now into the second half of the last lap (Semester VIII). The boys, needing a high which only some desi drinks could bring, would be seen holding one another. They would not be putting in any effort whatsoever to stop the tears from rolling down their cheeks as they sang aloud alongside the full-volume *Tum toh thehre pardesi / Saath kya nibhaoge* that had hit the hostel during this time.

The Boys Hostel lay to the farthest **East** in the campus and yet seemed bereft of sunlight amidst all tears and gloom. Who says the **Sun** rises in the **East**! Contrast that with the Ladies Hostel where there was euphoria and joy over the long, insane and ruffled **queues** that of late seemed to get longer. The queues getting longer had to do with those boys who had declared themselves *audiences* and not *queuers* at the onset of the Rourkela inning. What that meant was that the **19 queues** were for the kids, not for them, as they were well-off on that front. But either because these claimers were deserted in love or possibly because their initial claims were fake, they had also started rushing to the queues during the last lap (Semester VIII). **Result:** Queues were getting longer! So coming to the Ladies Hostel, on the whole there was shine and brilliance all around. So much so that Sun God chose the Ladies Hostel to shower His beams on. With even the Sun God showing partiality traits, the boys were up in arms, accusing louder than ever before that *partiality* wasn't a trait confined only to the mortals!

Enough was enough, and this unfairness on part of the Almighty had to end without any further delay. After all, the days were now passing quickly. And the shimmering line of the shore (end of four years in Rourkela) was just around the corner. It was a matter of time that **God** intervened to get the *law of averages* to set in.

The Snehas would often hear (not see) a horse's **trots**[10] in their dreams of late. If anything, it was a *sequel* in their dreams that had ignited reasonably long ago, around the time **DDLJ** hit the silver screen. Back then, however, the dream sounded a mere soft-footed horse's **walk**, nothing more. But having been preoccupied with flaunting the long queues outside their windows, the Snehas had chosen to ignore those **walks.** But not anymore. The excruciatingly mysterious **horse's trots** in their dreams were now getting way louder for them to ignore, indicating enough that the horseman riding the horse was no longer seven-seas away. What had up-until-now been an audio-only dream, was now preparing to show, albeit hazily. Very soon, the haze unveiled, showing a horseman whipping the horse on its way to the **Sneha**. Damn it, *Kuljeet* that was!

It was interesting how most DDLJ characters inspired the boys. **Raj** for reasons most obvious; **Simran** for reasons even more understandable; **Preeti** (Mandira Bedi) for getting the Rahuls to dream of

---

10 Reference: horse's gaits in the order of briskness are: *Walk, Trot, Canter*, and *Gallop*.

a queue that was forming at their windows instead; **Baldev Singh** (Amrish Puri) for having mellowed down in letting Raj win. **Baldev's** popularity in the boys' hostels stood next only to Raj. But what was equally interesting or maybe even more was that none of these characters impacted the Snehas as much as *Kuljeet's*. And this was because the *Kunwar Sahab* at the *Thakur wali haveli* which the Snehas accidentally overheard their parents talk about, smelled *Kuljeet* more than anyone else in the world! No wonder the dream sequel!

All in all, their parents were now setting their sights on Snehas' marriages – in line with '*bitiya badi ho gayi hei*'. When the Snehas overheard their parents talk about this, they were alarmed. Rahul—they fathomed for the first time—was better than Kuljeet! In short, God had heard Rahuls' prayers. Indeed!

And thus came that crossroad of life where Sneha had her most decisive turn to take. One road led to that highway where the *horse-trotting dream sequel* would end only after *Kuljeet* whizzed through the air on his horse to arrive at his destination which wasn't Sneha's. And the other led to Rahul who had no clue of how the four years flew. Rahul wasn't quite sure if the unit of **Electrical Inductance** was *Henry* or *Ford*, but remembered every calendar date all four years when Sneha didn't attend class. And on those days he would sit in the class, lost and doomed, as though the classroom were bare and lifeless. Rahul had lived to capture and freeze that moment when Sneha would nod a **yes** to his one most-rehearsed question, "Will you be mine?" Even if that meant him freezing along. Even if that meant he forgot his own name, let alone the unit of **Electrical Inductance.**

The years are long gone. But many summers into the end of the memorable REC Rourkela stint, not much seems to have changed. Given a chance to relive or redo the four Rourkela years, not one boy would choose a life any different. Because the hostel was one place where the size of pocket holes never came in the way of partying; where how unprepared you were for "tomorrow's" exam never came in the way of watching "tonight's" movie at the college AV Hall; where the feeling of struggling was just so temporary—thanks to the hordes of strugglers all around, every moment; where oxygen in the air was a mere formality, the boys enjoyed inhaling *uncertainty*. Here is that batch still preferring that air of uncertainty, smelling in it that whiff of winning. As they say, *uncertainty creates winners*. Meet the batch of **extraordinary winners**. Or was it the **extraordinary** batch of winners? Something still sounds amiss. Let's try one more time. "Meet the **extraordinary** batch of **extraordinary winners**." Now that sounds like **heaven**. Because that sounds like **ninety-seven**!

Welcome to the New World

Meri Naukri Lag Gayi Maa

The college ended in May'97. This was followed by a one-month break at home before we would join our new job. For those with jobs at the campus, this is usually the time when the parents are a mix of **pride** and **caution**. **Pride** stems from the fact that the son has a job in hand which he was so qualified enough for that the company came over all the way to the college to hand it over to him. **Caution** lies rooted in the belief that the air is replete with witches and witchcraft and that it may not be long before someone cast an evil eye to the feeling of joy in abundance. To thank the Gods—and this would also have to do with cutting the witches' ill-attempts to size—the moms would also include a prayer dose over and above the ones she has been doing for ages. Pretty much like the mobile phone booster recharge pack!

Those were not the times of live communication updates. Instead, those were the days of letters and posts. We exchanged a couple of posts across all others in the batch who would eventually reach Hyderabad to join *Satyam Computers*. Though belonging to a place reasonably far away from Hyderabad, Venu was going to be our anchor in Hyderabad. This was only because he was the lone Andhrite in the group. And after a rather slow one month at home—and 'slow' because we were eager to start our new job—we reached Hyderabad. It seems strange in today's time how people could contact one another at a new place during the times of no mobiles and no internet, but we did not miss one another in Hyderabad.

We reached the office the following day on what would be our first ever day in the office. A hotter receptionist and more beautiful decors we had seen only in movies. And though we boys were pretending to be all normal and not overwhelmed, our crocodile-like agape jaws said it all. What came over the next one week or so was all about inductions and corporate life and how it was so 'different from the average-class world outside'. The managers in formal suits spoke and implied—or maybe it was we who inferred—that "we may have been dazzled in this world of lights" but "that was nothing new for them!" *Free coffee from the vending machine, moving around the floors in elevators, formal wear, calling everyone by first names (no sirs or mudams)...* was it all real? We would pinch ourselves time and again lest we were sucked in the cosmos with no trace!

Many things were great, many others not quite. At a place where even the local-to-us Venu was a stranger to Hyderabad (Venu hailed from Ongole that was a good 400 km from Hyderabad), we were at the mercy of our karmas!

The realtor, Ram, would show us houses-on-rent. The one rental flat we 'agreed to' and 'moved into' took no more than 12 hours to make us all 'disagreeable' and 'move out of'. Very near to the Airport, every flight taking off from or landing at the airport would wake us up with its roar, and the night went into getting a feel of the aerial traffic at the Hyderabad airport. By morning—it was when we were all unanimous that we were vacating—we had a good whiff of how a landing flight sounded different from the one taking off!

We started our Hyderabad innings with very 'undernourished' pockets. There was a limit after all on how long our parents could support us. With expenses ranging from *most times plausible* to *at other times outlandish*, the only thing that grew in July '97 was the size of our pocket holes. The grand dreams of buying gifts for parents, friends and girlfriends alike had to be sedated for the time being with reasonably strong sedatives because the month of August when we would receive our first salary would go into firefighting and breaking even!

The first salary came and though that did not overturn the struggle overnight, the rain did bring some respite to the parched lands. We had some new sets of clothes and body language reflective of a pretension that we were not aware of everyone around in our neighborhood noticing us. All this declared that we had entered a corporate life where talking big was not that big a deal! We were undergoing the three-month classroom training full time which made the Hyderabad innings an extension of the REC Rourkela stay. Better classrooms; classes where you could also share jokes with the trainer; where thanks to the centralized A/C, you were oblivious to the heat outside; where you dressed like a gentleman no matter how unlike one you actually were and many more firsts differentiated these classes from those in the college. How the fun would extend to home at the end of the day in the office and how the best cooks prepared even better recipes, it was, as we recall now, a dream run! There were six of us staying together and though the home and kitchen set-up was getting better by the day, we were light years away from the most basic amenities. The most notable absentee was the LPG cylinder and stove. What we had instead was the electric stove that called for repair just about every day, thanks to the coil which somehow proved gentler than tender rose petals! A flicker of a voltage surge or a spoonful oil spill and the coil would give up! Slowly but surely though, we were getting more adept at fixing the loose ends and very soon that would mean that our rate of fixes was getting better than the surprises and challenges that would descend upon us. The train that had been limping on the National Highway up until the end of July, showed promising signs of making it to the tracks in August, with the passengers (six of us) hopeful that by September, the train might well start flying!

Gaurav, Nitesh and Atul were part of another group from REC Rourkela to have joined Satyam Computers in Hyderabad and they were staying at a different place. If July had left us pocketless, it could not have been very different for this group either. In all, the variance between dream and reality was in red for all, but for Gaurav, it went a shade darker! And when in August we got our first salary, his irony could not have been starker. Gaurav had to call home in the middle of the month (August) for some monetary assistance. Not because he was an ardent casino player but because he had sent a sizeable chunk of his first salary to his parents. This *act of bravery* was definitely inspired by Bollywood movies where the hero lays his first salary on his parents' feet. Gaurav, though, failed to read the disclaimer that comes alongside these moves: *All characters are fictitious and any resemblance to anyone is purely coincidental!*

Meanwhile, Atul was keen on getting better at scooter riding. Gaurav had got his old scooter from his hometown after he moved to Hyderabad. Very unfamiliar with the city and the colony—early days that those were, and those were not the mobile-phone days either—Atul did not return home hours after he had set out. Slowly but surely, the anxiety level of his roommates was bound to violate the threshold level. Concerned, the roommates set out to search for Atul. You can identify your car, scooter, or cow from a distance, no matter how ordinary it looks or functions. It was all dark when Gaurav saw his scooter coming towards him. But when it reached him, his heart was in his mouth to see that someone else was riding it. Thankfully though, before his heart raced out of him, he was relieved to see Atul as a pillion rider! While riding, Atul happened to completely miss contact with the 'control room'. Since he wasn't a well-versed driver and the fact that the scooter was a museum piece that even an expert driver would find difficult to ride, Atul requested a passerby to drop him at the address he read out. The passerby dropped him home safely!

All in all, to have brought a mini REC Rourkela to Hyderabad was a time to behold. We were subconsciously aware though that the dream run of fun that had got off in Rourkela close to four years ago was in its last lap and that once this get-together ended, life would be so very different. Today, I say to myself, "See, didn't I tell you?"

In Rome, be Roman

With the Rourkela baton in our hands in the form of the job that we secured at the campus placement, we reached Hyderabad. With all firsts—first job, first time in the city—we wore brave faces, hiding any show of anxieties as we were all set to start our sprint. Venu was the lone Telugu-speaking member in our group. No wonder, he was our leader by default.

We moved into a 2-BHK apartment and got ourselves into organizing the necessities—the kitchen and the bedroom in particular. Such luxuries like TV would not even have been on our agenda but for the cables hanging in the flat. Those were not the DSTV days; instead, local Cable TV operators serviced the cable television requests. As we calculated, the operators were yet to remove the cable TV connection from this flat after the previous tenants had vacated. No one amongst us was a TV freak, but our anxiety and disquiet would be evident when a cricket match involving India would be aired on a TV Channel. And the hanging cables were blatant reminders of the fact that we were only a TV Set away from watching the match live; the cable connection was already in place!

It was Sunday, and India was playing Pakistan. Those were not the cricbuzz.com days when you could get the score updates even before the ball was bowled! All we would know was that the match was in progress, with some intermittent updates. It would be from a passerby at times and at other times by peeping into a shop having a TV set where the match would be showing live. Manoj (Panda) returned from a haircut and told us all of the TV he saw in the salon. We deliberated over how we could bring the TV home. Mind you, we were good with the cables; all we needed was a TV! Sangram Shee, Venu, Manoj and I, each contributed Rs.500 and the idea was to request the salon guy to let us bring his TV home for the day. If he had any qualms about the idea, we thought we would go to the extent of tucking Rs.2000 into his pocket as caution money. Our calculation stemmed from the fact that Rs.2000 should cover an old, portable black-n-white TV. We already knew that India had won the toss and had elected to bat, which meant time was running out. We had planned enough; it was now time for execution.

Over the days, we had noted one thing about Venu. He talked to the people all around, only in Hindi. This was incredibly ridiculous we thought because, at the start of our Hyderabad inning, the rest of us (all three) had banked upon his Telugu speaking abilities to come to our rescue whenever the situation demanded. Before reaching Hyderabad, people had forced us into believing that down in South India; people from anywhere else couldn't survive if they could not find a way with the language there. And in Venu, we thought we had found that 'way'.

While we thought we were 'outsiders' by being not able to speak in Telugu, Venu thought he was an outcast by speaking the language so different from the locals. Venu hailed from coastal Andhra Pradesh where the variant of spoken Telugu was way different. In short, for the rest of us, all we knew was that the language spoken all over Andhra was Telugu. For Venu, it was as much different as diatomic O_2 is from O_3 (Ozone)! On this day, however, we believed that if we stood any chance of getting the TV home, it could only be with Venu's Telugu. For psychologically, if the Salon owner felt that we guys were thugs who had planned to run away with his TV, he would have Venu's Telugu to fall back on. It would make him believe, we thought, that at least one of the thugs was not from a very far away land.

The four of us led by Venu reached the salon in what we thought might sound like an 'indecent proposal'. For the request of the kind we threw at him, he was not sure if what he heard was correct. And Venu repeated. From his tone, expression, and conduct, Venu sounded the second most pious and godly boy in the entire evolution of mankind; the first being Lord **Ram,** and that was enough to run a smile over the guy's face. The rest of us stood like **Laxman**, **Bharat** and **Shatrughan** to make it look like it was indeed a call of the gods 'today' and to which the man must relent. He did! We pushed the Rs. 2000 into his shirt pocket, sounding like "*Ye toh aapko Rakhna hi padega.*" Venu had done his bit and it was for the rest of us to change hands in bringing the TV home. The portable CRT TVs of those days were far from portable and carrying it all along the way to the 3rd floor (our flat was on the 3rd floor) would not have been fun if the excitement over the India-Pak live Cricket Match had not blinded us as much as it had done!

The cable was hanging in the room but was it working? There was no easy way of verifying this unless you connected it to a TV. We had been silently praying all the way that the cable worked because we knew that if someone could make the orphan cable work today, it had to be God! It was time for light, camera, action. We inserted the cable pin into the TV; switched the TV on; twisted and turned a few knobs including the channel and we could hear something. Hurray! The cable was working. After a few more knob-turns here and there, we reached the channel where the India-Pakistan ODI was aired live. It took a while for the audio and video to reach reasonable levels. And we looked all set. But before our effort could make way for celebrations, we discovered that it was pouring in Nagpur where this match was taking place. Damn! We had asked God to make the cable work. We never asked Him to take care of the Nagpur weather. The day went into waiting for the rain god to fold up and go. Not to be. The TV remained on; so did the ground covers! The match was eventually abandoned.

We did not need Telugu speaking skills to return the TV. Nor did we need to trouble **Ram** for it. San**gram** instead volunteered to take this job, and when he returned with our hard-earned cash, all of Rs.2000, we were happy that not all went wrong on that eventful Sunday!

Aasman Se Girre, Jaane Kahan Atke!

Fresh from Engineering college and into your new job is when your *josh* to *hosh* ratio is at an alarming high. And one big reason for this stupidity—many a time the biggest—is that you think people all around are noticing you. You usually share your accommodation amongst three-four people and it used to be only boys or only girls during my time. For the boys, this gave an added reason to be funnier which they believed was daring!

After starting our new job, it had been close to six months since Yash and I were in Hyderabad with many other boys. And it was time to travel home (Patna). In Hyderabad, we took a train bound for New Delhi, named NDLC Express. Why did we board the New Delhi-bound train when our destination was Patna? The *lizard* train would sever its tail in Nagpur.

The tail happened to be the two bogeys bound for Patna. In Nagpur, another train from Mysore, bound for Patna, was supposed to add these two severed bogeys to its tail. The overall idea was pious: there being no direct train from Hyderabad to Patna, this arrangement ensured that if you were to travel to Patna from Hyderabad, you would not have to change trains after you boarded one at Hyderabad. Long story short, train A from Hyderabad to New Delhi would leave two of its bogies in Nagpur. And train B, from Mysore to Patna, would pick these bogeys up at Nagpur, and run all the way to Patna.

Train A arrived in Nagpur early in the morning. Yash and I assumed that the overall affair in Nagpur would take an hour, if not more. This included train A detaching the bogeys and train B picking those up. And daring that we were, we got down from the train. Early morning that it was, we took our time to brush; have breakfast; look around for magazines; have a cup of tea, etc. When we came back to the platform about 30 minutes or so later, we found the platform readying itself for the arrival of some other train. What? Where were those two bogeys? I had a habit of noting down in my mind the train bogey number I would board. Each train bogey has this number written in its middle when seen from the outside; it is usually a four or five-digit number. This train bogey number happened to be 5831. Nowhere to be seen, we inquired from the staff around. We realized for the first time ever that parents' and elders' advice to not get down from trains 'no matter what' was not about being old or

254 ✖ *Mera Bhi Proxy Maar Dena*

non-daring, but about being sensible! Train A was late that day. And Train B happened to reach Nagpur even before Train A had arrived. In situations like this, when train B arrived in Nagpur before train A did, train B would not wait to pick the tail bogeys of train A. Train A instead would continue to carry these bogeys with itself to Itarsi, which was a good five hours from Nagpur. We found that the next train to Itarsi was four hours later. This meant that we were at least nine hours away from Itarsi!

The one non-daring thing that we had done— and that happened to be the only sensible thing we did that day—was to chain our baggage in the train. This meant someone would have to break the chain to stand a chance of taking the bags away. That seemed to be the only respite in an otherwise 'replete with hopelessness' scenario we were in.

As we were traveling home for the first time after our first job, we were carrying gifts for friends and relatives. And with the bags carrying all these gifts traveling way ahead of us, we were at the mercy of fate! Besides everything else, Yashwant was also carrying a ring. He had announced loud and clear to his fiancée about it. He now wished that he had either not broadcasted it that loud, or such a small package that it was, he should have carried it in his pocket. But then, if wishes were horses... In the age of no mobile and no internet, it was *Ashirwad, Karma, Luck, Fate* and *Viswas*—nothing more, nothing less—that we could count upon to get hold of our separated bags.

We had lost hope that we would see the baggage again and even if we did, it was next to impossible that our contents would remain intact. When what you realistically expect is Earth and what you hope is Sky, you remember God the most.

In the four hours we had in Nagpur, we did all that we could to make *Ashirwad, Karma, Luck, Fate* and *Viswas* smile upon us! The Railway Control Room in Nagpur took our message with an assurance that it would be forwarded to the Railway Control Room Itarsi, but with no assurance whatsoever about the action that the Itarsi Control Room might take or initiate in response to that message.

Four hours passed in Nagpur and it was time for us to board some train that would pass by Itarsi. On the whole, we were *all over the place*. We left Hyderabad for Patna and we were in Nagpur; our luggage, on way to Itarsi!

When we were already at our lowest in the six months ever since we first reached Hyderabad for our first job, came another shocker. The train we boarded in Nagpur (for Itarsi) was a superfast train and the ticket we were carrying turned out not valid for this train. "You would be considered Ticketless Passengers," cried the TTE (Train Ticket Examiner).

We had reasons to believe that no matter how low and hopeless you thought you were, there could still be a lower and more hopeless situation in life! Life seemed to be teaching all lessons to us on the same day as though tomorrow would never come! We managed to get away with a soft penalty and this seemed to be the first good thing happening to us that day. 'Could this be the beginning of the end of all bad's for the day?' we desperately hoped.

Close to nine hours after train A had played spoiler in Nagpur, we finally reached Itarsi. And who says miracles do not happen? Train A had severed the two bogies in Itarsi (instead of Nagpur) and we understood that train C from Gandhinagar to Patna via Itarsi would carry these two bogies to Patna. I could identify the bogey number 5831 from a distance, placed in some desolate corner of Itarsi railway station, alongside the other hapless bogey. The bogeys were still waiting for train C to arrive in Itarsi. When we got inside the bogey, the fellow train passengers were relieved to see us back.

But alas! The Control Room message did not miss the Police that day. Before we reached Itarsi, the police had already relieved the baggage from the chain and the lock and taken them to the Railway Police Station, Itarsi. *Aasmaan se girre aur khajoor pe atke!* The next go-to place was the Railway Police Station, Itarsi. With the exchange of a few pleasantries, we could get all our luggage back, but not before convincing the police that the baggage indeed belonged to us!

The sight of the baggage and the fact that we were now in possession of those, got us to feel as though our Mt. Everest expedition was worth the effort! Having conquered Everest, it was now time to get back to the Itarsi Railway Station where the bride (bogey 5831) was waiting for the groom (Train C). But…

The Police station visit, freeing the baggage from the clutches of the police, returning to the Itarsi railway station all of these took no less than an hour. And this time was enough for the desperate *dulha* (Train C) to run away with the *bride* (bogey 5831) leaving the *baarat* (Yash and me) stranded!

We looked at each other and shouted out louder than we had ever done—as though to tell God that we were not just sorry now but angry too! Train A must have reached New Delhi; Train B, Patna; Train C would not have been far behind. But we were still in Itarsi, waiting for a train D that would get us to reach the moon. Yes, Patna had become moon if not sun that day. Overall, we were only 22 trains short of what could be the train Z to Patna!

Jhonka Hawa Ka Aaj Bhi

Looking at her, I would feel a blush brush gently painting every nook and corner in me with the silkiest of its bristles. From her glimpses that I would catch in the classroom seated a row diagonally behind, to her pictures I would click in my mind and would remain busy gazing when she would not be around, not a moment passed when she could be away. The occasional moments when her eyes would turn to notice me catching her glimpse would be witness to the beat or two that my heart would skip as every cell in me hummed in chorus to the most divine symphony playing within me.

This summed up the *pyar* (love) and *kashish* (attraction) story of the 'boys in love' in the REC

Rourkela batch of '97. Every love duet from *Kumar Sanu* and *Alga Yagnik* would get every boy to wonder how every song could mimic his state word by word! Studies had to take a backseat as the boys found so little time and mood for it. That was understandable because life is not about priorities; it is about what is more important 'now'. Studies had to wait.

It would take months of tryouts and rehearsals to get to that decisive evening when I would speak my heart out to her. And a day prior, a tornado of sorts would be blowing me apart. Will I? Will I not? Will she slap me? Will she cry? Will I collapse? The 101 questions as though coming from an interrogating agency within me would get me more nervous than a soldier surrounded on all sides having no escape route whatsoever. Less than 24 hours to go when I would tell her all. When I would be rehearsing the smiles and lines 'one last time' before leaving all to the Almighty, I would realize that my smiles weren't quite gelling with the flow of lines. The smiles that I would be rehearsing would be aimed at giving her the impression that I was not nervous!

Besides the interrogating agency, I would also hear a crowd within me calling me names; the most terrible of all being 'joker'! Smiles went awry and I would also go on to discover that my memory had started failing me big time and the lines that I had put my heart and soul into memorizing were just not coming right. "Damn, months of hard work as sincere as this would have easily gotten me into the top 10 in Electrical

Engineering if not three," I would hear something within me declare.

Nine-thirty at night already and the area around the hostel mess would be filled with loud sounds of empty cans and vessels, indicating that the hostel mess was winding up. I had been postponing my dinner by 'another two minutes' over the last one hour in the hope that I would be all set for tomorrow's test until I decided to skip my dinner: "a very small price to pay for a project as divine and holy," I would think. In some way, my unconscious mind would be calculating that skipping dinner that night could be that small offering that God may be interested in and who knows, it could tilt the scale in my favor! Oh, how difficult everything was. And they say Engineering is not that big a deal!

The calendar date turns to the D-day

It would still be fairly dark; sleep would be eluding me. Another 12 hours to go when I would tell her all, and I would conclude that I would be tossing and turning for the rest of the night until dawn. 'It was D-day and could well be the most historic,' I would feel like thinking. 'Will she blush at hearing me say all? Will she tell me she needed time to think and revert?' I would continue with all assumptions and conclusions I could draw: 'Obviously, she won't be frank enough to accept my proposal, but I would well take that response from her as a Yes.'

Smiling all to myself this moment and feeling thirsty the next as though the long-awaited verdict in a bank robbery case where I had been the prime accused was to be out today, I would bleed in cubes of white if cut. Yes, near-frozen I would be! Skipping dinner on any previous night would have elephants running in my tummy any other morning but today seemed just so different. I was not hungry yet. Had Ramesh not given me a shout for breakfast, I may well have skipped breakfast too. This would not have been as an offering. But because my mind had been preoccupied with so many other important thoughts, it failed to lend ears to the terrible cry of hunger emanating from my belly!

News from 'ground zero' at five o'clock in the evening

That February evening was warm and caring. Warm not just because it was making all arrangements to welcome Spring but also because in the first two minutes that I greeted her and spoke to her, I had well gone past all the time that I had conversed with her in the last 18 months, ever since we joined college. The air and the aura with the shower of fresh air would have easily injected bloom and blossom into the most sterile of plants today. But there I was, observing a steady decline of oxygen levels in myself. "And before I ran out of oxygen completely," I would say to myself, "I will tell her all." It would be time to come right on all that I had rehearsed for months.

"I have had something to tell you for a long time." The first line would come with misplaced smiles. I knew this would happen and yet could not set it right.

"But never could; or never got an opportunity to," I would continue. I would not be doing that great up until then. But the consolation would lie in the fact that the situation could have been worse if she had decided to not lend her ears at all; a possibility that had crossed my mind once if not more. The falling oxygen levels in me were now a *phoonk* (puff) away from dousing, and I let the last line go. "I am interested in you. What have you got to say?"

The 'ground zero' was an uninhabited area in the college campus lying farther west to the Ladies Hostel. The boys would usually fire their rehearsed-for-months lines here. So there I was, firing mine. Silence descended upon the hills all around as though what I had fired were not words but a gun! Had it been a movie shot, the view would be aerial, showing winds catching up and blowing with great speed, piercing the silence. "But I have considered you a good friend," would be the mortar coming from her in response, getting the wind to sound thunderous, busying the birds to rush for shelter!

In life up until that day, I had found something, somewhere that could come to my rescue whenever I ran out of plans. It could have been laziness to wake up early that cost me my breakfast but which I could still live with because the hostel or the college canteen would have something to offer. It could be my lack of preparation some other time that costed a good grade but that I could try making up in my next exam. It could be insincerity at home sometimes that upset my mom, but I would make amends for it to cheer her up. Not today. In the womb of nature, everything seemed exhausted. There was no line left to shoot. Smiles— mistimed and misplaced but showing up until then— had packed up, declaring that the show was over. The view would zoom out farther and farther from ground zero as though the camera had sensed that there was no view left to capture!

PS: This story is dedicated to every rascal in the batch of '97 who experienced a dip in oxygen levels during the four years of his Rourkela stay. For all others, you should have done better!

Never compromise on fun. It is the pathway to success.